Barnabas: Encouraged to Live

The Barnabas Chronicles
Book 14

By

Ronna M. Bacon

Trust in the Lord with all your heart and lean not unto your own understanding.

In all your ways, acknowledge Him and He will direct your paths.

NKJV

Table of Contents

His hand wrapped around his mug of coffee, Barnabas Carey padded through his apartment in the Barnabas Foundation building, his bare feet smacking almost silently on the dark hardwood floor. He sighed, his free hand scrubbing at his face. He felt every bit of his age of early thirties that night, the last four days wearing him out beyond what he had ever experienced. He stood for a moment in his home office, staring at the pile of files and personal mail his secretary, Amy, had stacked neatly there. Tomorrow, he thought, I'll look at them. Tonight, I just can't do it. He wandered over to the window, parting the drapes to stare out into the twilight, looking up at the darkening of the sky, watching the twinkling of the stars appear and the full moon shedding its light over the property. He could see the parking lot from where he stood, and counting cars, felt comfortable that all the men who lived there and were employed by the Foundation were at home with their ladies.

He turned, heading back for the kitchen, to refresh his mug of coffee before he stood, hand on the counter, his head turning towards the hallway. Fresh mug of coffee in hand, he headed for the living room, pausing a moment to scan it out of habit. It looked the same, he thought, just as it did a month ago when I left on the long-overdue vacation. His eyes dropped to the couch and his face softened before he moved forward, mug landing on the table beside it before he sat, his eyes on the lady who slept, curled up, her head on her arm along the back of the couch. He gathered her close to him and heard her gentle sigh as she settled down in his arms.

Barnabas studied the dark red of the curly long hair, his hand brushing down it, knowing that the deep brown eyes would be covered, eyes he felt he could drown in. He sighed himself, his head of heavy black curls cropped short dropping back on the couch, as his thoughts wandered. His dark blue eyes closed for the moment. He had no idea how to approach what he had to do. He had briefly spoken with his father when he had arrived home but didn't let him in on the secret he had brought with him.

He dozed off, his head rising as he heard a tap at the door, and then shoes being nudged off and set neatly by the door.

"Barnabas?"

"Yeah, Breck?" He heard his lifelong friend and second in command head for the kitchen.

"When did you get in?"

"About four or five, somewhere in there."

"I didn't see you come in, but I saw your truck as Neasa and I were heading out for dinner." Breck lifted the coffee pot and stared at it before he dumped it out and made fresh. "How old is this coffee anyway?"

"I think I made it when I got in. I've been drinking it. But I could use a fresh mug."

"You sound exhausted. Didn't you relax at all? That was the whole point of you going away by yourself."

Barnabas shook his head, even though Breck could not see him. "I did for a bit. The last couple of weeks were rough."

Breck could hear something in Barnabas' voice, not too sure on what. He doctored their coffee the way they both liked it, and picked the mugs up, intent on heading for the living room, when he paused, a sudden deep urge to pray for his friend. Somehow, he knew that when he entered the living room, things would change for them. Lord, I have no idea what I'll find going on with my friend, but You do. You have gone before us in this. I pray for him. He's worn out, has been for a while. He's been there for each one of us, all thirteen of us, as we went through what we did. Now, we need to be there for him, without knowing why. Lord, bless my friend. Protect him. Heal him.

Breck padded to the door, intent on not spilling the coffee from the mugs he had filled almost too full. He set the one down on the table by Barnabas' elbow, a quiet thank you from his friend before he stood, freezing as he did so, seeing the lady wrapped in his friend's arms, her hand clutching at the dark blue T-shirt he had changed into after his shower and shave.

He backed away, finding the chair he preferred, his mug setting down a little harder on the table beside it than he had thought. He stared at his friend, waiting for him to speak.

Barnabas' head had gone back on the couch, his eyes sliding closed, so he missed Breck's initial reaction. But he heard the silence from his friend. The silence that asked questions that Breck would not or could not ask aloud.

"Breck?" Barnabas looked over at his friend without raising his head.

"Barnabas? What's going on? You didn't have a lady in your life when you left. At least I don't think you did."

"I didn't. Not really. I left to find her, to see if she was all right. She wasn't and I had to step in. I had no choice. God would not let me walk away without trying to help her."

"Does she have a name?" Breck's head tilted as he stared at her. "She looks familiar. Do I know her?"

Barnabas raised his head to stare down at his lady before he nodded. "You do. It's Aubrey."

"Aubrey Dorsett? That Aubrey? I thought you had forgotten her."

Barnabas shook his head. "No, I never did. I couldn't. She was the only one for me. We kept in touch for a few years, and then about two years ago, I stopped hearing from her. Letters were returned unopened. Emails bounced back. Phone calls went to a disconnected number."

"She didn't want to stay in touch."

Barnabas shook his head again. "No, that's wasn't it." He looked down as Aubrey stirred, her hand reaching up to rub at her nose before she laid it back on his chest. The soft lighting glinted off the rings on her hand.

"Wait. Barnabas, she's wearing a wedding band and engagement ring. What is going on?" Breck's voice died away as Barnabas lifted his hand, showing his own wedding band. "You didn't, did you?"

Aubrey roused even more, her head raising as she squinted, hearing another voice.

"You awake, sweetheart?"

"Not really. I thought we were here alone. Who do I hear?"

"Breck."

"Breck? I don't know a Breck, I don't think."

Barnabas shook his head at Breck. "You do. We were all friends at university. Don't you remember?"

She thought and then nodded. "Breck. I do. Why is he here?"

"He lives in the building, sweetheart. He dropped by just to make sure we're okay."

"Oh. Okay. Wake me in the morning, please." She dropped back to sleep, her head tucked up under Barnabas' chin.

Breck had listened in wonder as they had talked before he looked at Barnabas, seeing not just the fatigue but the stress, strain, and worry that had overcome him.

"Barnabas, I know you have a story to tell. Tonight is not the night. We'll meet in the morning." Breck stood, hesitating for a moment.

"Thanks, my friend. It is a story to tell and it's not over. We're on the run. I haven't slept in four days, just trying to get back here without being followed."

"Barnabas? Four days? Where did you come back from?"

"Northern Ontario. It's not that long a trip unless you're being tailed by someone who really wants to stop you and will stop at nothing to do that, including murder."

Chapter 2

Rousing the next morning, Barnabas stared around the living room, surprised to find himself still there. He squinted at the clock on the mantle and sighed. His parents would be there shortly and he wasn't ready to face them. Not quite yet. The lights were still on, he saw, and he shifted Aubrey enough so that he could rise and shut them off, returning to stare down at her before he simply gathered her close and walked to the bedroom. She roused as he did so, a hand rubbing at her eyes.

"Barnabas?"

"It's okay, sweetheart. Just moving you to the bed."

"No, it's okay. It's morning and I need to be up." Her head went back down on his shoulder as she yawned. "What is on for today?"

"I'm not sure. Mom and Dad will be here shortly."

"They will? I have wanted to meet them for so long. I think I met them briefly."

"You did, our first year at school. Things have changed over the years." Barnabas set her on her feet. "Go on and shower, have a bath, whatever it is that you want." He frowned. "But I don't have stuff for the bath for you."

"It's okay. I'll manage." She was reaching for the clean clothes that they had purchased, turning to find him handing her a pair of scissors to cut off the price tags.

Barnabas hesitated, seeing the sadness that she was trying hard to cover up, as well as the fear. He wrapped her in his arms, a kiss delivered before he prayed for her.

Aubrey looked up at him, a smile hovering on her face. "Thank you, my love. I think I felt your prayers over the years, particularly when things were the roughest. They kept me going."

"You have never been far from my heart or my prayers, sweetheart." He watched her closely.

"Breck was really here last night?"

"He was. He's married now, a lady named Neasa. She's what he needs in his life." Barnabas grinned. "She rides a motorcycle."

"She does? And he loves his motorcycles. A perfect match." Aubrey turned away. "We need to talk some more, my love, but for now, I need to get ready to meet your parents."

Barnabas wandered back to the living room, opening drapes as he did so, to tidy up the couch area and then carry his used mug back to the kitchen. He set fresh coffee and put the kettle on for tea for his mother, a smile crossing his face at the anticipation of how she would react to his bride. Lord? Aubrey needs a mother. Please let Mom be that to her.

He searched the fridge, finding fresh vegetables and juice and eggs. An omelet, he decided, reaching for the frying pan that he preferred for that. Turning as he heard the door open, he knew his father had appeared. His parents had an apartment on the upper floor of the building and had just recently moved back to the area to live permanently.

"Son?" Bruce Carey's voice carried through the apartment.

"Kitchen, Dad. Coffee's ready." Barnabas wiped his hands on a towel and turned to find his father standing beside him, reaching to hug his son, holding on just a bit longer than he normally did.

"Good to have you home. You didn't call much." Bruce's keen dark blue eyes studied his son, seeing the changes the last four weeks had wrought in him.

"No, I didn't. I was on the move a lot, Dad." Barnabas pulled his upper lip over his teeth, a move that Bruce recognized as uncertainty on his son's part.

"Barnabas? Do we need to talk?"

The younger man nodded. "We do, Dad. We do. But it involves someone else, not just me." His head turned as he heard soft footsteps approaching the doorway.

Bruce turned to face the door, stopping in stunned silence at the beautiful woman who appeared and stopped, uncertainty on her face as well. Barnabas sighed and moved to draw her into the room, an arm wrapped tight around her, just as he heard his mother enter.

Elizabeth Carey moved to the kitchen, not seeing her son for a moment, setting down the baskets of muffins and biscuits that she had brought. Finally turning, she looked first as her son and then at the lady in his arms.

"Barnabas? What's going on? You didn't have a lady in your life when you left." Her brow wrinkled. "At least, I didn't think that you did."

"Mom. Dad. This is Aubrey Marie Dorsett Carey. She is my bride and the love of my life." Barnabas was not watching his parents, his eyes on Aubrey as he introduced her, finding her watching him. He reached to kiss her before he looked over at his parents.

Elizabeth stood, her hands over her mouth, surprise on her face for a moment. Bruce had hidden his surprise but interest stood on his face.

"Your bride? Your Aubrey? The lady that you used to talk about and then stopped?" Elizabeth moved around the table, coming to stand with her hands on Aubrey's arms as Barnabas tightened his around his bride. "Oh! You are so welcome to the family. We have waited for all Barnabas' life for you." She simply swept Aubrey into a tight hug.

Aubrey, surprised at first, reached to hug Elizabeth in turn, finding the mother welcoming her to the family in such a way that she knew she was loved and wanted already. Barnabas stepped back, his father at his side, an arm around his son's shoulders.

"Pulled a fast one on us, son? You had your reasons, that much I know."

"I did, Dad. I had to." Barnabas sounded like a little boy for a moment, trying to explain to his father what he had just done. "She was in danger, Dad. I had to rescue her."

"And brought her to us. We'll help you, son." Bruce slanted a glance at his son, a smile hovering on his lips. "Off on your own adventure?"

Barnabas groaned and then nodded. "I am, Dad. I have been for the last four weeks. The past five days or so have been brutal. We'll talk."

"We eat. We pray. And then we talk. Is this why Breck has called a full building meeting for this afternoon in the chapel?"

Barnabas' head shot around as he stared at his father and then nodded. "He dropped in last night. We didn't get much time to talk. I figured that he'd do that."

Elizabeth had turned, her arm around Aubrey, listening before Bruce moved to stand before Aubrey, his eyes kindly and welcoming before he too hugged her.

"Mother, it seems as if you now have the daughter you always wanted. Love her lots."

"Oh, I already do. I don't know what happened, son, but your bride is a welcome part of our family." Elizabeth moved past her son, a hug given to him before she began their breakfast preparations.

Barnabas moved back to wrap Aubrey in his arms, finding her shaking.

"All right, sweetheart?"

"I think so. I didn't expect this."

"You are now a loved and special part of our family. And there are thirteen men and ladies who have been waiting to meet you for years."

Her head shot around as she stared at him. "That many?"

"That many. The building family. And then there's Doc and Anna as well as Amy, my secretary, and her husband. You have been prayed for."

Chapter 3

Her hand tight in Barnabas', Aubrey stood in the hallway outside the chapel in the Foundation building. She had had no idea that the building was that big or that so many people called it home. He had tried to explain it to her, finally just telling her that he was giving her a tour of it. She was suddenly afraid for him and for the ones in the building.

Bruce and Elizabeth had found their seats inside, listening to the talk and laughter of the men and ladies they considered family. The men, other than Breck were all orphans, brought to the Foundation by Barnabas from all provinces and territories. Most of the ladies were as well, but the ones who weren't gladly shared their parents and siblings with the others. Elizabeth watched as the little ones that were starting to grace the building chattered away or sat staring at the chapel, given their ages.

Bruce leaned over. "They have no idea, do they?"

"Not at all. I know that they have prayed for a help-meet for him. I fear for him, Bruce, and for his Aubrey."

"I know. He didn't say much but I can feel the concern and fear that is driving him to do what he has done."'

Barnabas studied Aubrey, finding her discomfort coming through. She has no idea, Lord, what I am about to walk her into, and I did try, I know I did, to prepare her. She just wasn't ready for this. Forgive me, Lord, if I rushed ahead of Your plans, but You seemed to be leading in it all.

Aubrey's hand brushed down the soft yellow tunic that she wore over a brand-new pair of brown corduroy slacks. She had fled her home with very little in the clothing line and Barnabas had taken her shopping, insisting that she buy what she wanted as well as what she needed. She could never remember doing that, she thought. Her eyes found his, trust in him in hers, before he bent to kiss her and then pray for her.

"Are you ready, sweetheart?"

"I guess. I'm not good at this. I haven't been around people since we graduated. He made sure of that." She grew angry at how her life had been impacted by her guardian.

"I know, sweetheart. I know. We're working on that for you. These fellows in there?" Barnabas nodded at the door. "They will work their wonders again, and we'll bring him to justice. They have done it for all of them."

"All of them?" Aubrey's eyes grew huge. "All of them? Even Breck?"

"All of them. Even Breck. Some were so close to death, it was touch and go. Burnie's wife actually did die and had to be brought back. Bradon was drowned and revived. God is with each one of them, sweetheart. They will welcome you."

"If you say so." Her hand tightened in sudden fear. "I hear babies."

"You do. God is blessing our building family with little ones. We will do everything we can to protect each and every one sitting in that room." He paused, praying for them both before he reached for the door and opened it quietly enough that no one heard. He led her into the chapel, standing at the back, finding Breck watching for him. Breck nodded and rose, standing at the lectern, finding all eyes on him as the room quieted.

"Buckley, before we start, we need you to pray, and in particular for Barnabas."

Buckley rose from where he sat beside his wife, Locklin, and did that. He had been their church minister until the Barnabas Foundation board had asked him to take on a new ministry. He sat when he finished, his eyes on Breck, sensing the concern that Breck was trying hard to hide.

Breck searched each face, finding interest and concern on them, his eyes stopping on each couple, before he looked at Doc and Anna, and then Bruce and Elizabeth. He drew a breath of relief. They've met her, he thought. They've met her and welcomed her to the family. They have the daughter that they wanted so badly, but God had other plans. His eyes raised to Barnabas, finding his friend watching him steadily before they moved to Aubrey, finding her watching Barnabas, confidence in her groom and her love for him on her face.

—

"Fellows. Ladies. We have been through a lot in the last few years. I don't need to remind you of that. You lived it. God brought us through and has strengthened us in Him. We are now able to reach out to others under the mandate of the Foundation and be the encouragers that were envisioned when it was set up.

"About four weeks ago, we sent Barnabas off on a long-awaited and much-needed vacation. You have all asked over those weeks if I had heard from him. He was not in contact a lot, but that was okay with us all. We understand that as our leader, he needed the time away.

"Barnabas returned late yesterday afternoon. I dropped in on him last night. A situation has occurred with him, that led to our meeting today. He didn't call the meeting. I did, out of concern for him, and so that we could all be on the same page in praying for him." Breck stopped, biting at his lip, unsure of how to proceed.

"Before any of you look around, Barnabas is standing at the back of the room. He is off on an adventure, my friends, just like we all did. When he was away, he found the lady, the love of his life, that he lost touch with. I know the lady and I can safely say that they are two parts of a whole. They complete each other." He paused once more. "Barnabas, please? Bring your lady love forward and introduce us to her. And then, you need to share what adventure that you are off on and what we can all do to help."

As Breck sat beside Neasa, Barnabas strode forward, confidence in his very step, Aubrey keeping pace with him, her eyes on the front, her hand tight in his. He stopped and turned to face the building family, searching each face, his eyes lingering on his parents, before he looked down at Aubrey, finding her face tilted up to him, uncertainty in her eyes, even as her face remained calm. He simply bent and kissed her, sealing his love for her in the presence of their friends.

Chapter 4

His eyes raising to search his friends, Barnabas drew a deep breath of relief. He found no censure on their faces, only interest and concern. He sought his father, finding Bruce watching him intently, and then nodding. Bruce knew, without being told, that Barnabas had been in difficulty the last few weeks, and that on his own, other than for their God. He wished that it had been different, but he trusted his son.

Aubrey's hand tightened on his for a moment before Barnabas began to speak.

"I need to apologize for not keeping in better touch with you all. I just felt it best not to. Not that it seems to have mattered. The one responsible for separating Aubrey and me all those years ago has been tracking us.

"First, let me introduce you to Aubrey Dorsett Carey. Breck, Aubrey, and I were friends in university. Breck, I'm sorry. You never knew how much Aubrey and I meant to each other. We didn't realize it ourselves until the last few weeks of university. Through circumstances out of our control, we were separated. We managed to keep in touch until about two years ago. At that point, my letters, emails and phone calls went unanswered or were returned or bounced back on the server. I didn't feel that I could walk away from any of you, not while you were going through what you were. When Breck married, I knew

---

the time had come to go find out if the lady I loved had moved on or was still waiting for me." He paused his eyes on Burnie, who was frowning. "Burnie, it's going to be like one of those mystery stories that you write, and the adventures that you all underwent which you tell us are more bizarre than one of them."

Barnabas turned to Aubrey, seating her beside his mother, who simply wrapped an arm around her new daughter. His father's hand rested on his shoulder for a moment before he returned to the front, to lean one elbow on the lectern.

"This may take a while, but I'll give the shortened version. Fellows, I need you to work with me. I have been in touch with Dallas and he'll be out tomorrow as he's away today." Barnabas swallowed hard.

"Four weeks ago, I hit the road and travelled up north, many hours and many miles up north, to a small town where I knew Aubrey had had her home. I didn't know if she was still there or not. I rented a small cabin in a neighbouring village, not wanting it to seem obvious that I was a stranger there. I went back every day, searching for her. I finally ran into someone who has been concerned about her. That person showed me where Aubrey was living. This was five days after I arrived there.

"I searched for the house, finding a huge, opulent place, that I knew was not what the Aubrey I knew would have wanted. I walked the perimeter, watching for her, and not seeing her. I had no reason to doubt that she wasn't there. There was security all around, which seemed odd at the time.

—

"Finally, on the sixth day, I was able to approach the house, finding no guards around. I knocked and then tried the door, finding it opening. I shouldn't have entered, but something drove me forward. I searched, finding a room on the main floor that was locked."

Barnabas had turned the key, opening the door slowly, not sure what or who he would find inside. He stepped through the doorway, searching, hearing a soft cry and then a body hitting him, arms wrapping around his neck. He felt the tears that soaked into his shirt.

"Aubrey? Is that you?" He couldn't get her to raise her head to look at him.

"Do you know how long I have waited for you? I thought that you had forgotten me." She sniffed as she tried to control her sobs.

"Never, sweetheart. Never. I thought that you didn't want anything to do with me."

Aubrey shoved away from him, anger sparking in her eyes. "What did he do? Can I leave with you?"

"That's why I am here. What do you need to pack?"

Aubrey ran for the closet, pulling out a backpack, and blindly stuffing it with the bare minimum of what she wanted. She had had months and years to plan this and knew exactly what to take. Barnabas frowned as she pulled out the drawer on the bedside table and reached to the back of the table to pull on a packet.

"My identification." Her simple statement said a lot. "He tried to take it from me, but I hid it." She ran back towards him, a hand reaching for his, watching as

---

he closed and locked the door. "He's away for a few days. When he's away, no one is here, only long enough to bring me cold food and water."

"You've been a prisoner?" Barnabas ran with her towards the trees, his eyes watching for someone coming to stop them.

"I have been. Since I graduated. The last two years have been the worse." She ducked down into the back of his truck, letting him pull a blanket over her.

"Stay down, Aubrey. I'm heading for the cabin I rented as if I'm heading back there for the night, but I have everything with me. I'll drop off the keys inside. That was the arrangement. Then, we'll find somewhere that we can talk."

Chapter 5

Aubrey finally sat in the front seat, brushing back her hair, turning to look behind them. Barnabas had sped away from the cabin that he had rented, even though it was still early morning, heading for a nearby city. He knew that they couldn't travel as they were. A plan had come to him, only he wasn't sure that Aubrey would be agreeable. They didn't know one another anymore.

"Barnabas? Now what?" Aubrey turned to him.

"I'm heading for the town nearby. We need to talk, Aubrey."

"I know. I need help to bring him to justice. Only I don't know how to do that."

"I can help. I have many friends and lawyers who will help." Barnabas pulled into a fast-food drive-in. "Let me grab us some food and something to drink, and we'll talk."

Their meal finished, Barnabas gathered the garbage and headed for a waste container, standing and staring at it before he angrily shoved the debris into it. Lord, I am so angry and heartbroken for her. How do I keep her safe? I see only one way, and I'm not even sure that is what You want for my life. He sighed, turning back to the truck, sliding inside.

Aubrey watched him closely, before he reached for her hand, his head bowing as he prayed for them

---

and for her. He knows, doesn't he, Lord? Without me saying anything, he knows.

Barnabas' thumb rubbed at her hand, and he spoke without looking at her.

"Aubrey? I have a plan, a plan that would bring you away from here, but it would also put you into more danger.'

"A plan?" Aubrey's hand tightened on his. "Does it involve more than you just riding in on your white charger and taking me away from there?"

"It does." He finally looked up at her, his heart in his eyes. "I have loved you for so long. Even when I thought you wanted nothing to do with me, I loved you. Will you marry me, Aubrey? Today?"

She stared at him before she had to blink away the tears. Her voice was barely audible as she spoke.

"Do you know how many nights that I have dreamed of that? That you came and saved me, swept me away to your town, married me, and brought him to justice?" She swiped at the tears on her face, taking the handkerchief that he handed her. "Yes, Barnabas. Yes. We were at that point when we graduated, I think. Only he stepped in and took over."

"He did. And we will talk about that. Now, let's see where the city hall is."

Two hours later, Barnabas tucked Aubrey back into his truck, sorrow at the fact that she had a rushed wedding weighing him down. He stood for a moment, watching her through the window before he moved to slide behind the wheel.

"Where to, Aubrey? Where can we go that he can't find you?"

"Go north a ways. There's a small town that he avoids. He was forced to leave it about five years ago." She watched as Barnabas parked at a small bed and breakfast.

"We can stay here likely for a day or so if they have rooms. Let me find out."

He was back shortly, driving around to the back of the building. "We have three days here. Then we move on. I don't have to be back at work for about three weeks."

"You don't?" Aubrey was surprised.

"No. I took a four-week vacation, intent on finding you." He grinned at her. "And I did."

"And you did." Aubrey stood in the room that they had been assigned. "This is nice. I love the white and green."

"You always liked your green." Barnabas swept her into his arms. "Still do?"

"I do. He decorated in browns and grays and blacks. I had no choice in what he did." She leaned back. "Barnabas, I have few clothes. I didn't bring what he made me buy or bought for me."

"I know, sweetheart. I know. Let's spend some time in prayer. We need it. And then we'll go find you some clothes. And a nice restaurant."

A week later, Barnabas shuddered suddenly as he shut the back door on the cab of his truck. We've been found, he thought, even moving from town to town as we did. He helped Aubrey in and then ran for his side, sliding inside.

"Barnabas?" Aubrey shot him a look and then her eyes moved to the outside. "He's found us?"

"Someone has. We need to move. I'm heading for the eastern side of the province. From there, we'll work our way back towards Lake Erie and home." He grinned at her. "Have I told you today that I love you?"

"You have. I will never tire of that. I love you, too." Aubrey watched the traffic behind him. "The white truck. That's his son's. How did they find us?"

"I should have taken off for the south. They figured that we'd stay up this way. It was a chance that we took." Barnabas abruptly turned into a parking lot, the horns of the vehicles behind him sounding, and then drove through it to emerge and head the way that they had just come. "I hope that I can shake him long enough to get away. He has no control or authority over you?"

"He hasn't since I was like eighteen. He just refused to relinquish it. I was able to send documents to another lawyer in your town, hoping that word would get to you."

"And because of lawyer/client confidentiality, they couldn't."

"His name is John. I remembered you talking about him."

"John? One of our Foundation lawyers. Wonderful. We'll go see him once we're home."

—

Chapter 6

Five days before he had to head home, Barnabas stood on a street corner in a large town, Aubrey's hand tight in his. He felt it tighten and looked down, seeing fear on her face.

"Sweetheart?"

"His son. He just drove past us. He saw me, Barnabas."

He simply ran her across the road, dodging traffic and shoved her into the truck. He was behind the wheel and driving off, his eyes watchful. They had made a habit of not staying more than one night in a motel or bed-and-breakfast.

"We'll stay just outside of town tonight. It's getting late to be moving too far." Barnabas finally pulled into an out-of-the-way motel.

The next morning, they were up and gone earlier. Barnabas drove back and forth between cities, towns, and villages for the next four days, his eyes watchful, not able to sleep. His eyes were heavy but he refused to give in. Aubrey worried, but kept watch with him, sleeping in fits and starts, on the lookout for her guardian or his son.

Driving towards home, Barnabas drew a breath of relief. Here, he thought, Aubrey will be as safe as we can make her. I'll take her in to see John, to find out what our options are. He sighed. He had to introduce her to his parents and then the building family. He would not find censure from any of them, that much he knew. There might be questions but they would only be to ensure that the couple was safe. Then, the fellows would start their investigation, that much he knew.

Barnabas parked in his designated spot and sat for a moment, before he reached for Aubrey's hand, his head bowing as he prayed for them, as a couple, and for her, that they could quickly resolve what was going on and find out the reasons why. He walked her towards the patio of his first-floor apartment, her eyes taking in the three-story building. Unlocking the door, he swept her up and carried her inside, claiming a kiss as he set her down in his home office.

"Let me grab our bags and I'll be right back. Go on. Take a look around your home." He was out to the truck, and back in, depositing the bags into the bedroom, before he turned to find her still standing in the office, her eyes on him.

"You haven't moved." He walked to stand in front of her, reaching for her hands.

"No, I didn't. You need to do this, Barnabas. You need to show me your home, and then we'll make it ours."

He nodded. "Of course. Here, let's start in my office." He led her from room to room, listening to her comments, smiling as she took delight in the rooms.

They prepared a quick meal before she headed to shower and change, finding her way back to the living room. Barnabas stood watching her before he handed her the cup of apple spice tea that she seemed to have developed a liking for.

"Will it do?"

She set her cup down and spun in a circle. "It will more than do. You saw the house that he had. It wasn't mine. I had that small room for the last two years. Even before that, I only had access to two rooms beside mine. The kitchen and the laundry room. I wasn't allowed in any other rooms." She flopped down on the couch, her hands rubbing at her eyes. "I'm exhausted, Barnabas."

"Curl up there and sleep, sweetheart. I'll be back in about ten minutes or so." He watched as she curled up on the couch, an arm along the back as she studied the room. "And we will make changes here, sweetheart, to make this your place as well."

Aubrey nodded, her face thoughtful. "We will, my love, but I need to live here first to get a sense of what we want. And it will be our decision, not mine."

Barnabas came back to the present, his eyes finding Aubrey as she sat, his father's arm around her, her hand in his mother's. Thank you, Mom and Dad. You have taken her to your hearts. She needs this. He looked down, not wanting to look at his friends. He jumped slightly as he felt an arm on his shoulders and Breck began to pray for him and his Aubrey.

"Fellows, we have a mission now." Breck looked around the room, finding the silence greeting his words comforting. They had all been through too much to be surprised at what Barnabas had said. "First, we greet our newest family member. Then, we make plans."

<hr>

Buckley was on his feet, heading for Barnabas.

"First, we pray for Barnabas and his Aubrey. Then we make plans. Locklin has already whispered to me that we need a pot-luck tonight, to welcome Barnabas back and to welcome his bride." He prayed for his friends before he hugged him and then stepped back, watching the couples move forward. Aubrey had simply risen as he had begun to pray, to come and stand beside Barnabas.

Chapter 7

Aubrey stood that evening, watching as the ladies scurried around, setting out the meal before she walked forward, her contribution in her hands.

Berneen turned as she approached, reaching to take the hot pan of scalloped potatoes from her, setting it down before she reached to hug her.

"You are so welcome to our family, Aubrey." Berneen watched her. "We have prayed for you, without knowing you."

"You have?" Aubrey nodded as she thought through the words. "Barnabas said that you had been. We still need those. To find my guardian and his son? That's what we need to do. But why do I keep calling him my guardian?"

Cadee moved in, hugging her as well before she linked an arm with her. "He's not, is it? How many years?"

"I would have been eighteen or so. I was that before I graduated from university. He tried to play it that he was my guardian longer. I found the paperwork one day and took it."

"You did?" Devaney hugged her as well. "And where is it?"

"Barnabas' lawyer, John, has it. I haven't heard from him, but nothing got through. That's why Barnabas came looking for me." She looked up as the ladies grouped themselves around her. "You need to introduce me to you all, with your fellow's name. And the little ones."

Hagen nodded as she stood beside her, her son in her arms. "And we will. Right now, we eat and enjoy our fellowship. We try and do this once a month, just for fun." Her son had been watching Aubrey and suddenly launched himself at her, his arms tight around her neck before he leaned back and then moved in to give a sloppy kiss.

"I'm so sorry, Aubrey. He never does that to people that he doesn't know."

Aubrey was laughing, hugging the little fellow, who refused to look at his mother as she reached for him. "It's okay. I'll keep him for now, if you like. It's been a long time since I've been around little ones. I used to help in the nursery at church."

Barnabas reached for the little fellow as well, the little boy never refusing to come to him. He watched in amazement as the little one buried his face against Aubrey and just refused to look at anyone else. Brandon stood there as well, his daughter in his arms, who as soon as she saw her brother, launched herself from her father towards her brother.

Aubrey's face lit up with laughter as she held the two little ones, her face covered in sloppy kisses.

"I never expected this kind of welcome." She looked up at Barnabas. "You didn't warn me, my love."

"No, I didn't. They've never done that before."

—

Hagen and Brandon finally removed their twins, much to the dismay and protest of the little ones. Barnabas stood with an arm around Aubrey.

"I think they're in love, sweetheart."

"Maybe. They are so sweet." She looked around. "Okay, so what happens now?"

"Buckley prays. We dish up, find seats, eat and have fun." He looked around. "I have wanted my bride with me here at these dinners for so long. I'm glad you are finally a part of it."

"I am. And tomorrow, we meet with John?"

"We do. I sent him a message that we were home and that you were with me. He's been trying for years to reach you, he said."

Aubrey wandered the apartment late that night, restless, unable to settle down in one room. Her hands reached to touch the ornaments that Barnabas had sitting around. She knew that he was on a call, that he had been reluctant to take, but felt that he had to. She ended up in his office, his hand reaching for her as he paced.

"Dallas will be out tomorrow afternoon." He tucked his phone into a pocket.

"Who's Dallas again?"

"A detective with the force here, and a good friend. He's worked with all the men and ladies." Barnabas began to laugh. "I didn't expect the twins to do that."

Aubrey's face lit up. "I don't think their parents did either. It's not the first time I have had twins fighting over me. I have missed the little ones."

Chapter 8

His keen eyes on the couple across from him, John Tyson assessed them. They're in love, I can see that, Lord. Now, how do we keep them safe? I know of this man who claims to be her guardian. He will stop at nothing to regain control of her, even declaring her incompetent and having mental health issues.

"John? You have read through what Aubrey sent you?"

"I have, Barnabas. He is not your guardian, Aubrey. In fact, he was never your guardian. He had no control over what you did. Your mother was your guardian. I understand that she died just as you turned eighteen?"

"She did. He stepped in during my grief for her and just took over. I didn't fight him. I was too heartbroken. When I did question him, he waved off my objections and concerns."

"I see. He has drawn up papers, with your grandmother's purported signature, stating that he was to be your guardian until you turned thirty. That was two years ago?"

"It was." Aubrey stared at him before the anger grew in her. "That's why."

"Why what?" John had a good idea but he needed her to say it.

"That's why he imprisoned me. It was the day before my birthday. He just shoved me into that room, despite my protests, and locked the door. It was a lock that could only be opened from the outside." Aubrey's face dropped into her hands. "I didn't have my phone with me. He had taken it. That's when he cancelled the email, cancelled my phone, returned any letters that came to me. I had very few of those anyway."

Barnabas' arm was around her. "What now, John? You know my guys are working on this."

"That I know. Breck has already been in touch, not to ask any questions specific to you, Aubrey, but in general." He looked down at his notes. "I'll have these transcribed, Aubrey, have you sign the statement that you have given me, register it at the court. We will need to have someone assess you, just in case he plays that card."

"Oh, he will. He's already told me that." Aubrey looked frustrated. "But who?"

"We know a lady, who is a respected forensics psychologist, even though she's retired. She'd be around your age. Darcie's not from the area, so that will help."

"Anything. As soon as possible. He's not going to wait." Aubrey sat back, a puzzled look on her face before she turned to Barnabas. "I don't know why he's done this. He would try and get me to meet with different people, said he was trying to help me get established as a singer. I had no interest in that. You know that."

"I do. You have a beautiful voice, but that's not where you want to serve. John? What next?"

"I'll contact Darcie and see what she can arrange in the next day or so. She has always been willing to work with the Foundation. She and Doug are supporters. That may put a wrinkle into it, but I don't think it will." John stood, his hand out to shake Barnabas' before he hugged Aubrey. "I have no doubt that he will try his best to trap you somehow, and take control of you. But legally? He has no standing at all. This paperwork shows that. When we go to court, and that we will need to do, he will be sent away. It's not legal. Do you have anything of your Grandmother's showing her signature?"

Aubrey nodded. "I do. I kept things hidden from him, receipts, bills, letters, addresses. I'll make sure that you get them."

"Good girl. You've a head on your shoulders, despite what you went through." John watched them walk away before he reached for his phone, asking to speak with the Chief of Police, Will Peters.

"Will? Got a moment?"

"I do. Just a moment, John, while I close my door." Will sat back into his chair after closing his door. "You've called. You have a concern."

"I do. It's young Barnabas."

"Barnabas? I thought that he was away on holidays."

"He was. He's been back three days. The thing is, Will, is that he married while he was away. His

———

42

bride is one that Jeremy Forester has tried to force into the music scene. He gave her paperwork that said he was her guardian until she turned thirty."

"Still trying his old tricks? We've been trying to catch him for years, just never had the proof."

"We have it now. Young Aubrey was smart enough to remember my name from her talks with Barnabas and sent everything that she could find. I am sure that she paid for that. He locked her up two years ago and cut off all communication with her."

"He did? Now, we can get him. You're worried."

"I am. He has already threatened to have her declared mentally incompetent. We went through that with Neasa. I prayed that we didn't have to again."

"Me too. Darcie's onboard?"

"She's my next call. I can't see her refusing. Barnabas mentioned that he had called Dallas yesterday and that they were to meet today."

"Good. I'll find him and speak to him. Anything else?"

"Not offhand. I'll make sure your people get copies of what she has sent. He's a mean, vindictive man. I fear for young Barnabas."

"There's that. I'll have a talk with him. Married, is he? Good. What's she like?"

"A very beautiful redhead, who is clearly in love with her fellow. They're parts of a whole, Will."

"Is that so?"

—

Chapter 9

Dallas stared at Barnabas that afternoon when he had tracked him down to his home office, not quite sure that he had heard him correctly.

"I'm sorry. I thought that you said you were married. You weren't dating anyone."

"I am, Dallas. Aubrey is the one I found in university and then we were separated, through no fault of ours. We had kept in touch for a number of years until all contact was cut off about two years ago."

"She did that? Then why marry her?" Dallas was puzzled.

"She didn't. A lawyer claiming to be her guardian did that. I've talked to John, and I can almost guarantee you that he talked to Will."

"He might have. Will was looking for me earlier, but I was out of the office. That could be what he wanted." Dallas ran his hand through his hair. "So, what do we do, Barnabas?"

"First, you meet my lady." Barnabas had his hand out to draw Aubrey to him. She had appeared in the doorway of the office and hesitated about entering. "Dallas, this is Aubrey, my bride and the love of my life."

Dallas turned to study her, finding her brown eyes watching him carefully, a calm expression on her face.

"Aubrey? I am glad to meet you, even under these circumstances. Barnabas, it was to stop with Breck, didn't we tell you that?"

Barnabas began to laugh and had to control it before he could turn to Aubrey, her puzzled eyes shifting between the two men. "We have told each fellow that it ends with the one before him. It never worked." He grinned at Dallas. "You're next, aren't you?"

Dallas looked horrified for a moment before he grinned. "Don't think so. I'm not part of the Foundation building family." He turned to Aubrey, sobering as he did so. "We need to get as much information from you as we can. Barnabas, here or in your office downstairs?"

"Here. And John has all the information that Aubrey could give him. He said he'd send it to you, but I would ask legally for it. It's another lawyer that we're dealing with."

"It is, is it? Makes no difference." Dallas pulled out his pad and pen. "Okay, let's get started. The sooner we solve it, the better it will be."

Two hours later, Barnabas closed the apartment door after Dallas. Leaning back on it, his head dropped forward and his eyes closed. Lord, this time, it's different. It's my lady, my sweetheart, who is in danger. And we don't know why or who all is after her. It can't just be that lawyer. Dear Lord, protect her. Help me to be the one who can do that, with Your strength. Please, Dear Lord?

Aubrey watched him before she just moved into his space and into his arms, her head resting against his chest. *Lord, protect this man who loves me. I know that man will go after him. I couldn't handle it if he is hurt because of me.* She leaned back as she felt Barnabas move.

"You're back to work when?"

"Tomorrow's Sunday, so it will be Monday. Are you ready for church tomorrow?" He assessed her, a frown on his face.

"As ready as I ever will be. I haven't been to a church service or heard a sermon in years. He wouldn't let me. I think he was afraid that someone would help me. He couldn't take a chance on that."

"No, he couldn't." Barnabas turned her and headed for the living room, sitting in his favourite chair and drawing her down on to his knee, cuddling her close. "We're not fancy dressers if that's a concern."

She shrugged. "I wondered. I was just going to go by what you were wearing." She bit at her lip. "I need to get some more things, Barnabas. I only have the basics."

He nodded. "As my wife, you will receive a wage from the Foundation. All the wives do. But that doesn't matter. The ladies will want to take you into town, introduce you around and find some outfits for you." He began to grin. "Hailey and Hollie, Hagen's twin sisters, have likely already talked Breck into taking them to town to do that. They have done it with all the ladies after Hagen and Brandon married. He's

---

like a big brother to them. They have him twisted around their fingers.”

“They will? How sweet? And I saw a younger man there, with Berneen, I think it was.”

“That’s her brother, Darbie. He likely went along with the twins. He says he hates shopping but he’s always up for a trip.”

“He is? You have such wonderful people here. I like how you found all orphans for the men. And to share your initials? That had to be God.”

“It was. I would be given a list, pray over and then find the one God directed me to. They are all different, have different occupations, and all volunteer. The ladies either work, volunteer, or are in school. Some are staying home now that they have a family.”

“That’s good. I remember you saying that the Barnabas Foundation was set up to be encouragers. I can see that. But where do I fit in?”

“Right now? They’ll go easy on you, seeing as you’re the new one here. It’s up to you what you do. I would like it if you kept track of the ladies. Neasa is doing that, but you can as well.”

“I don’t want to step in and take over. That’s not me. How be I focus on the little ones?”

Barnabas tilted his head to study her. “I don’t know that we ever really discussed that, as a Foundation board. There will be a play area and a playground going in. There is also an empty room on the main floor with outdoor access. Let me talk to the board. I am sure that we could turn it into a daycare

---

centre of some kind. I remember that you studied that as well as your business degree."

"I did. And I think that's what Jeremy was afraid of. That I would move on and away and he would lose a source of income that he was trying to establish."

Chapter 10

A week later, Baird stood and watched Aubrey as she wandered the gardens, a frown on his face. He realized that every time he saw her, she was on her own. That's not right. I know the ladies are great friends, but they have never shunned or ignored one of them. He turned, heading for the building, finding Berneen in the lobby.

"Berneen? Have any of you ladies talked with Aubrey? Every time I see her? She's on her own."

Berneen flushed. "I have been, Baird, but she's so quiet that it's hard to get a feel of what she wants."

"And the others?"

She shrugged. "I have no idea. They're not saying."

"This is not right, Berneen. She's part of our family, as Barnabas' wife. She was isolated for years, locked up for two. It has to be difficult for her to make the move that would make friends."

"You're right." She moved into his hug. "I'm sorry. I know better."

"You do. You know what it's like to be locked up." He reached for her hand. "Do you have some time right now?"

"I do. Where is she?"

—

"In the gardens. Come on. Let's go find her. I'll stay for a while and then I have to run. Invite them for supper if you want."

Berneen hesitated for a moment before she approached Aubrey.

"Aubrey?" She waited until the other lady turned. "I need to apologize. I was not the friend that you needed. Baird tracked me down. I'm sorry."

"For what? I could have made the motion to get to know you all. But you seem to be such good friends, I didn't want to intrude."

"Oh, Aubrey? Is that what you think? It would be no intrusion. We just open up our group and take in the next lady. Listen, we're meeting in about half an hour for Bible study. Did anyone ask you?" Berneen bit her lip as Aubrey shook her head. "I am so sorry. I know better. I should have asked you. Forgive me?"

"What's to forgive? I could have approached you. I just don't know how to anymore. Jeremy kept me confined for so many years. The last two I had no contact with anyone but him, or one of his security men if he was away."

Berneen reached to hug her. "That's so sad. I was kept prisoner for a few months until Baird appeared there as a prisoner. He made sure that I came with him when five of the men swooped in and rescued him. Listen. Let's head to Cadee's where the study is. And I know Hagen's sisters have things for you. They finally talked Breck into taking some time yesterday to go shopping for you. He's been running around like crazy the last week or so. And I think Darbie said he found something for you. Let's stop by Hagen's first and then head out." Berneen linked an arm with her. "From now on, if you don't speak up, I'll be your mouthpiece. I do that very well."

"You do? I never would have guessed." Aubrey bit back a grin as Berneen stared at her. "And I do want to hear about all of your adventures. Barnabas has told me bits and pieces. And he says that you ladies go into competition with the fellows to solve the mysteries."

"We do." Berneen tapped at Hagen's door. "But we all feel as if there has been something left hanging and unresolved."

"That could be, Berneen." Hagen stood in her open doorway. "Are you two coming in or are you going to continue your conversation in the hallway?"

"Coming in. Aubrey was wandering around by herself. Baird found her and then found me. We need to do better, Hagen."

"Yes, we do. I was heading your way later, Aubrey, with what the twins and Darbie found. Now that you're here, let me find the stuff, as Hollie so elegantly calls in."

Late that afternoon, Aubrey stared down at the bed, her hand covering her mouth, as she counted the outfits, sweaters, bath stuff, as Hollie called it before she reached for an eagle statue that Darbie had insisted she needed. She blinked back tears. Lord, it had to be You, to direct him to something that means so much to me. Eagles always were my favourite. Teach me to live again, dear Lord, and teach me how to fly above the storms.

Barnabas' arms came around her at that point and she leaned back against him.

"Lots of loot, as Darbie says." He grinned at her.

"The twins. Apparently, Breck had to free up some time yesterday." She held up the eagle. "Darbie found this."

"Your bird. You always wanted to try and find them, didn't you?"

"I did. Berneen and Baird asked if we would come for dinner. I didn't know what to say."

"We can go, or we can stay at home. It's okay. They understand." Barnabas was distracted for a moment.

"Barnabas?"

"Hmm? Sorry. There was a letter that came today in the mail. I need to go over it with you, but I think, if you're willing, we head for Baird's. We don't need to stay too late."

Chapter 11

Late that evening, Barnabas stood in front of Aubrey, an envelope held out for her to take. She stared at it and then up at him, shaking her head.

"I won't, Barnabas. I don't want to read what he has to say."

"You need to, sweetheart. We both need to know what he's up to. He's very specific. He knows that we are married. How I would like to know."

"Someone from that town, likely." She finally reached to take the envelope as if it were poisoned. "Do I really need to?"

Barnabas swept her into his arms and then to a sitting position on the couch in the office.

"You do. If you want, I'll read it for you."

"No, it's okay." Aubrey shook her head, extricating the letter and unfolding it. Her face hardened and paled as she read. "Is he for real? He never said anything like that before. He was always very careful about how he worded anything."

"He's seeking revenge. They don't care how they talk." Barnabas tapped the letter. "This here? It's a direct threat to our lives. I'll give a copy to John and the original to Dallas."

"How do we stop him? I can almost guarantee you that he will have gone into hiding."

"Likely. We'll be careful, as we always are. Dallas will likely want to speak with you again, to see what new information you can give him."

"He picked my brain clean the other day. I don't know of anything more that I can tell him." She leaned against him. "Is this what the others went through?"

"Much worse for some."

Aubrey sat in silence, staring down at the letter. "How do we protect one another?"

"That we will work on. I know the fellows have started their investigations. Don't ask me how they find their stuff. They do. They all search differently from each other." Barnabas began to pray, his voice echoing through the room.

Aubrey finally rose and began to pace, her arms wrapped around herself. Barnabas watched her before he reached for his phone, which had been vibrating. He stared at the number before he just let it go to voicemail.

"Barnabas?" Aubrey sat beside him, leaning over to look at the number. "Jeremy? He has your number?"

"He does. It's on the website, so he could find it." Barnabas set his phone to one side. "I'm not listening to the voice mail. I'll do that when I see Dallas. I am sure it's not going to be nice."

"How do we do this, Barnabas? I feel like a broken record." Aubrey sighed. "I don't want to bring any harm to the ones here or to the little ones."

"I know, sweetheart. I know. For now, we continue as we are. We have to live our lives. We can't hide in fear."

"I know that. He wants us to. That's what that letter is all about. He tried so hard with me to make me fear him. I never did. I was disgusted by him, angry. I couldn't understand at first why Mom would have done this. Then, I realized that it wasn't Mom. It was him. And I don't know why."

"You don't? No trust funds? No land coming to you? No property?"

"Nothing. I had scholarships and grants to go to school. I worked during the summers to help pay my way. And I worked part-time when at school." Aubrey sighed. "I just don't know why."

"We'll figure it out." Barnabas wrapped an arm around her, praying for her as he pulled her close to him. "Now, then. What have you decided about the apartment?"

"The apartment? Where did that come from?"

Barnabas shrugged. "I guess that I just want you to feel at home here. Make it yours."

"I am at home, Barnabas. I would be at home wherever you are. I am not sure what you would like to change. The furniture? It's great. The floors? I love the hardwood. The walls? They are the colours that we talked about, all those years ago."

"I know. I think I decorated it for you. But there has to be something you would like to add."

—

55

"Right at the moment? I can't think of a thing." Aubrey snuggled down beside him. "There are holidays coming up. What does the building do for Christmas?"

"In years past, we would have a dinner on Christmas, but that has been changing. Some are at relatives, those who have them. The others? It's hard to say what this year will be like."

"Do you decorate the lobby?"

"You know, we never really have. How be you work on that? The ladies will likely help." Barnabas paused, not quite sure how to phrase his next question.

"Berneen made sure that I was part of the Bible study. I need that. They are all wonderful ladies, a little unsure of my role here, though. I think that is why they are hesitant to approach me. After all, I am married to the boss, as they say.'

"True, but not true. I oversee them, through Breck. I work for the Foundation more than I do oversee them."

"I know. It's just complicated. That's all."

Chapter 12

The next morning, Aubrey stared at the security guard as he tried to hand her a package. She shook her head, pointing back to his desk. She had been studying the lobby when he had approached her.

"I didn't order anything. And I have no one that would be sending me anything." She paled. "Please. Put it down." She peered at the writing as he did so. "It's what I thought. I need to contact that Dallas. Do you know how to?"

"I do. Barnabas warned us to expect things like this, but I don't think we expected anything so soon." He turned away to call and then turned back to her. "Barnabas isn't in this morning, is he?"

"No, he had a meeting in town, he said, that would likely take him until noon." Aubrey backed away from the desk. "I don't want to even know what's in it." She almost ran from him, stopping in the centre of the lobby, arms wrapped around herself as she stared at the door. I could make a getaway, couldn't I, Lord? I could run, change my name, my appearance, but he would still find me. That much I know. She jumped as she felt a hand touch her arm.

Brandon stood there, a frown on his face. "Aubrey?"

"Brandon? He's found me, do you know that? He sent that package over there." Her finger stabbed towards the security desk.

"He has? He did? We need to call Barnabas and Dallas." He reached for his phone.

"Barnabas is not to be interrupted. I won't allow it. He's in meetings all morning."

"He would set them aside for you. You do know that?"

Aubrey nodded. "I know. Right at the moment, I am not in danger. It's a threat, just like the letter last night. And that Dallas has already been called."

"He has?" Brandon looked around. "Then, you're running away. It won't work. Barnabas would just come after you. It would put you both at risk." He pointed towards a hallway. "Come with me. I'm heading to the conference room that we use. We've been wanting to speak with you about this man."

"Don't get me started. I know too much and I don't know why." Aubrey frowned as she entered the room. She paused, studying the work stations, the kitchenette, the whiteboards on the walls. "You have it set up nicely. Does it work?"

Brandon grinned at her. "It does. We've found more information than what we really knew we could. We also have a friend who researches stuff, as Benen calls it, and finds information that no one else seems able to."

Aubrey wandered the room, her eyes taking in what had already been added to the whiteboards. She

—

stopped in front of one and then smiled. A logic problem, she thought. How interesting!

"That's Burnie's idea." Benen spoke from behind her. "He set it up for Buckley, I think it was, and we used something similar for him, Breck, and now Barnabas."

"I find it interesting. What does Burnie do?"

"He's a mystery writer."

Aubrey spun, her eyes huge. "A mystery writer? Oh, I have always wanted to meet one."

Benen grinned. "And now you have. Aubrey, Barnabas has given us what he can. But we always like to speak with the ladies. Sometimes, they can add to what we know. They also have a different perspective than us fellows."

"Our brains work differently, is that what you're saying?" Aubrey sighed. "I can give you what I know. Right now, I am waiting on that Dallas to come out. There was a package delivered to me this morning. And Barnabas had a letter yesterday."

"We have that letter. Not a very nice fellow, is he?"

"No. And I can't figure out why. Barnabas asked last night about any inheritances. I have none. Mom scraped together what she could after Dad was killed in a motor vehicle accident when I was twelve. We never had a lot. Dad's insurance had to pay for our upkeep. I have no idea how Jeremy got involved, but he suddenly just appeared in the days after Dad's death. He wouldn't leave. Mom asked him to many times. When he was around, she made sure that I wasn't."

"Your mother knew something? And she left no papers or diary?"

Aubrey shook her head. "No. I cleared out her desk and paperwork when she died. There was nothing other than receipted bills. I used her insurance to help fund my schooling." Aubrey grew pensive. "I just don't understand."

Benen drew a chair out and made her sit, moving away for a moment and then returning with a cup of tea for her.

"Here. Cadee told me that you like this tea. Drink it." He drew out a chair beside her, his mug of coffee landing on the table before he reached for a pad of paper and pen. He grinned. "Breck has us doing this, reaching for pen and paper."

"He does? Is that what he always does?" Aubrey leaned her chin on her upraised hand, elbow on the table. "Talk to me, Benen. Tell me about you fellows. I know that you are all orphans, from every province and territory except this one."

Benen did just that, his pen moving across the paper as he made notes for her. When he finished, he tore the papers from the pad and handed them to her.

"Some homework for you." He grinned again. "I hear the ladies and you were together yesterday."

"We were, Benen. And it's hard for me. I have been so many years with just my own company."

"We know that, Aubrey, and we are praying for you and for Barnabas. You're the person who completes him. Even going through what you are, I am glad you are here." He raised his eyes as the door opened. "And there's that Dallas, likely looking for you."

Chapter 13

Filling a mug with coffee, Dallas drew a deep breath. He had to talk with Aubrey but Barnabas wasn't there. He wasn't sure how to approach her, given what she had been through. And now this, he thought. A box with dead roses and a sympathy card for Barnabas.

"Dallas?" Aubrey stood in front of him, worry on her face.

"Aubrey? Can we sit?"

She shrugged, heading back to where she had been seated and taking her seat again.

"What did you find?"

"Dead roses. A sympathy card for Barnabas." Dallas watched her closely, seeing her pale.

"A sympathy card. Was it signed?"

"No, just had his name on the envelope." Dallas pulled out his phone, bring up a picture with the envelope and then handed his phone to her.

"That's his writing." Aubrey shook for a moment before she thrust the phone back at him. "What's his game?"

"Your life." Dallas watched closely as Aubrey paled even more. "You escaped him. He wants you dead. And why? That's what we need to discover. And if he can't get to you first, he will go after Barnabas."

"I know. I know that. I shouldn't have left with Barnabas." Her voice was barely a whisper.

"He wouldn't have left you there, Aubrey. Not a chance on that." Dallas looked up as the door opened and nodded. He had reached out to Barnabas, who had responded with shock and then fear.

Aubrey jumped as she felt arms come around her and her head turned. "Barnabas? You were in meetings. They weren't supposed to call you."

"And do you think that I would sit in a meeting, knowing that you were being terrorized? As soon as the board found out, they sent me to you." Barnabas looked over at Dallas. "Anything else?"

"Just what I told you and the picture that I sent. He's upping his game, Barnabas. He's going to get more and more vicious as time goes by."

"I know that he will." Barnabas pulled out a chair and sat, Aubrey's hand tight in his. "What do we do?"

"For now? Take extra precautions. We can't find him or I would bring him in to question him." Dallas was frustrated. "If you see him at all, Aubrey, don't approach him. Call us."

Aubrey watched as Dallas rose and walked away, leaving her with Barnabas' arm around her.

"Sweetheart? Did you open the box?"

"No. I refused to take it from the security guard. He called Dallas." She turned to watch him. "I'm scared, Barnabas. I am so scared that he will try and hurt the people here. Maybe I should just leave."

—

"And I would leave with you. That would mean that we would be on our own. Here, we have our friends to help look out for us. I know. I know what you are saying. I feel the same. So did every one of the fellows and the ladies as well."

"They did? Then, how do we do this? How do we stay safe and keep them safe?"

Blair hesitated as he approached, not wanting to interrupt. Aubrey looked at him with a frown before she turned to Barnabas.

"Blair?" Barnabas peered over Aubrey's head at him.

"Barnabas. Aubrey. We found some information on your father, Aubrey, that we would like to speak with you about." Blair was still hesitant even as he spoke, bringing a frown to Barnabas' face.

Aubrey spun to stare at him. "You do? What is it? I have trouble remembering my Dad, it's been so long." Her face grew sad.

"We found this. Is this your father?" Blair handed over a photo.

Aubrey took it, staring down at it before her finger moved to touch it. She blinked back tears.

"Oh, Dad! I miss you." She blinked back tears even as Barnabas' arms held her. "Blair? Where did you find this?"

"In a newspaper archive. It seems that your father was well respected in his occupation as a contractor."

"He was. He never let any of the trades do shoddy work. If he felt it was, he made them redo it. He never wanted to be associated with any building that would be condemned or collapse. He had seen that happen." She looked up. "But I don't understand. Why this?"

"It's what we do, Aubrey. We look into everyone in your family, tracing what we can. We research everything we come across, no matter how minute. We confer with one another, bounce ideas back and forth. We will keep you updated. We will keep coming back and asking the same questions, different questions, whatever it is we need to do."

"They all look at it differently, I think I told you, sweetheart. It's how they work."

Aubrey was on her feet, moving towards the door, the picture of her father still clutched in her hands. She swiped at the tears on her face before she almost ran for the lobby, stopping to stare around. She walked quickly towards one of the two seating areas, drawing a chair up near the gas fireplace. Dad? Why? God, please? I need answers. I need to feel Your presence and right now, I don't.

Chapter 14

Neasa watched from where she had just walked in before she moved towards Aubrey, sitting in a chair near her, just waiting. She finally handed Neasa a handkerchief.

"Aubrey?"

"I'm okay. Blair found a picture of my Dad. I miss him so much." She held out the picture.

"This is your father? He looks like a kind and compassionate man."

"He was. He was." Neasa didn't realize that she had repeated herself. "To lose him like we did broke Mom. She was never the same. I still think that she died from a broken heart."

"That may well be. Aubrey? What can I do for you?" Neasa watched her, kindness on her face.

"To tell you the truth? I really don't know. I have been so isolated for so long, my social skills are rusty, if not non-existent. Jeremy saw to that." Aubrey studied Neasa. "How do I do it, Neasa? How do I get back to some semblance of who I was?"

"You'll never be her again, Neasa, unfortunately. That was taken from you. But you can become your own person once more. We are praying for you. We have been hesitant to approach you, not sure of just how to, knowing what you have been through."

Aubrey nodded, her eyes on Barnabas as he stood near the stairs, his eyes on her. She knew that he was praying for her. She could feel the prayers. "I guess that I would just come up and talk to me. If I'm quiet, it's not that I'm upset or don't want to be friends. It's just that I don't know how to converse with anyone anymore. I had two years of strict isolation. Before that, eight years or so of semi-isolation. I never saw anyone but Jeremy, his son, and his security guards." Her voice died away. "I wonder how much the fellows have looked into the son."

"I'm sure that they are." Neasa looked up as Jaxcy and Imly approached. "Jaxcy. Imly. You two look like you're on a mission."

"We are. Cadee has an idea of what we can do for the shelter inhabitants for the holidays. It means shopping, though."

"It does? Aubrey, you up to doing some shopping?" Neasa looked over at her.

Aubrey shrugged. "Sure. Why not? When?"

"Tomorrow. We're all available and so are the twins. Darbie is insisting that he needs to go with us. That we need a man with us." Jaxcy laughed. "He thinks that we can't defend ourselves."

"Even with the fire hose trick we used on Dan and his henchman?" Neasa laughed, picturing the scene. "Aubrey, you should have seen it. My step-father had appeared, had taken Breck down, the men and Dallas surrounding them. They didn't dare move in as one of Dan's men had a gun held on Breck. We separated into two teams, used the fire hoses on them, and knocked them down. It was a sight."

"It was, and it was good for you, Neasa. You know that as well as the rest of us." Imly reached to hug Aubrey. "I'm glad you're here, Aubrey. Barnabas needs you. We have all felt that he needed that special lady, and we just didn't know who."

"You did? He didn't tell me that." Aubrey seemed surprised. "Even though I have brought danger with me?"

"Aubrey, we have all done that. Some of us more than others." Imly simply shook her head. "We have learned to enjoy life, no matter how hard. The love of our men keeps us going. They try to protect us. Sometimes too much."

"Ain't' that the truth." Jaxcy grinned. "So, all day tomorrow? Or is that too long?"

"Let's start with the morning and see how it goes?" Aubrey suddenly yawned. "I'm sorry. All of a sudden I am exhausted."

"As you should be. We'll meet in the morning. Wear comfortable shoes." Neasa reached to hug Aubrey. "Have a good night, Aubrey."

The three ladies walked away, stopping to speak with Barnabas, leaving him laughing at something they said. He approached Aubrey, crouching down beside her.

"Okay, sweetheart?"

"I am. I'm sorry that I ran. I just couldn't stay."

"We know that. Your emotions will be all over the place. We understand. Ours have been too. Just don't run from me. That's all I ask."

Aubrey's hand rested against his cheek. "I won't. I can't, not even if I tried."

Chapter 15

Late the next afternoon, Aubrey shut the apartment door behind her and then leaned back against it for a moment. She stared down at the bags in her hand. She hadn't planned on buying anything, but the thirteen ladies, the twins, and even Darbie had insisted on finding things for her. Finally putting a stop to it, she had laughed and then shaken her head, telling them that she would never wear all the clothes that they seemed to think she needed. She grew sad as she thought of how she had only had one pair of jeans, a couple of sweaters and some summer shirts for the last few years.

Toeing off her shoes and then setting them tidily into the clothes cupboard near the front door, Aubrey headed for the bedroom, dropping her packages, pulling off her jacket and then heading for the kitchen. She needed a cup of tea. Squinting at the clock, she sighed. Barnabas would be home soon, she thought, and she had nothing yet ready for supper. Some wife she was, she thought.

Hearing the entry door open and close and then his footsteps, Aubrey sighed again and closed her eyes. She just couldn't do it, she thought. She was not a cook. That much, she knew. Neasa had figured that out early that day and had promised to come to help her. Neasa had been a trained chef before she married Breck. She had refused to return to that line of work, telling Aubrey that she just could not do that but she was ready and willing to help a friend in need. Was Aubrey a friend in need, she had questioned, a huge smile on her face as she did so.

Barnabas watched from the doorway for a moment before he moved towards Aubrey, his arms coming out to draw her back against him. They stood like that for a moment, his head resting against her. Aubrey felt her tension relaxing and leaving as it always did when she was near her love.

"Have a good day, sweetheart? I checked here at noon and didn't find you."

"I did. The ladies are a great group. The twins and Darbie are a riot, you know."

Barnabas gave a soft laugh. "That they are, considering that they went through a lot with their sisters." He didn't speak for a moment. "Anything happen?"

"No." She thought a moment and then shook her head. "No, not that I can put a finger on. I know I was being watched, just couldn't see anyone."

"That's what he is doing. Watching. Hoping to spook you. Trying to rattle you." Barnabas kissed her cheek. "It's Friday, sweetheart. How be I take you out for dinner tonight?"

"Really? Like we used to do?" She twisted in his arms, her own going around him. "I dreamt of those days so much that I began to look at them as just that, dreams."

"You did? I missed them. Casual or dress?" He let her make that decision.

"You don't care?" She searched his face. "No, you don't. How about casual tonight? I don't have the energy to dress up."

"Then, let me change from my dress clothes and I will be right back." He leaned down to kiss her, not letting her go until she shoved at him, a smile on her face.

Barnabas reached for Aubrey's hand as they walked across the parking lot to a local family diner. It was a favourite of his. He had been at school with the daughter who now ran it for her parents and knew that they would enjoy whatever meal that they decided to get.

Eva looked through the door and then held it for Barnabas, reaching to hug him before she studied Aubrey.

"Barnabas? Who is this lovely lady that you are holding so tight to?" She grinned at Aubrey.

"This is my bride, Aubrey. This is Eva. Her parents had this restaurant when we were growing up. We used to congregate here after school and on weekends. They never chased us away, always interested in each one of us."

"Hi." Aubrey smiled shyly at Eva. "It's good to meet you. Barnabas used to talk about this diner. He always was going to bring me here."

"Then, I am glad he finally has. Your booth is waiting for you, Barnabas. I'll be back with your coffee and menus. Aubrey, what would you like for a beverage?"

"You don't happen to have an apple spice tea, do you?"

"We do. I'll bring that to you." Eva watched as Aubrey slid onto to bench seat, Barnabas sitting beside her.

Her mother stood watching. "Who's that with Barnabas?"

"His wife, Mom. He's married. Her name is Aubrey. Didn't he and Breck used to talk about a friend named Aubrey?"

"They did. Wonderful. He always had a certain tone in his voice when he talked about her. She's the reason that he's never looked at another lady."

"That would be it, Mom. Like all the building guys. They're one-lady fellows, and each has found their lady."

"Just as you found your fellow, Eva. God leads us to that one."

Barnabas shifted uncomfortably towards the end of the meal, his eyes searching the patrons in the diner. He frowned as he studied the younger man sitting near the front, in such a way as he could watch their booth.

"Aubrey? Jeremy's son? How old is he?"

"About our age. Why?"

"There's a man around our age watching us. I wonder if it's him."

Aubrey leaned against Barnabas just enough that she could see. "It's him. That's Jason. We can't even have a meal."

—

"We can and we will. We will continue to live our lives, sweetheart." Barnabas sent up a prayer for protection. "You're finished?"

"I am. How do we escape? Through the kitchen?" She smirked at his look.

"Good idea. I would like to introduce you to Eva's parents. I know that they're usually here on a Friday night." He stood, reaching for her had as she did and then leading her towards the kitchen. He could feel the eyes on his back.

Eva's husband, Jim, a patrol officer, took one look at Barnabas' face and reached for his keys.

"Stay put. I'll bring your truck around front. And who is it that you're concerned about?"

Chapter 16

Aubrey shifted on the truck seat, looking through the back window before she faced front again. She was on edge, knowing that Jason had been in the diner. She was suddenly afraid for Barnabas but didn't know how to tell him that.

"It's okay, sweetheart. I'm scared too." Barnabas reached for her hand. "Jim will have a talk with him, find out why he's here."

"He will?" Aubrey turned to study Barnabas, as much as she could see him in the dim lighting.

"He's a patrol officer. We were in school together as well. He was a close friend. We're not as close as we had been. Time and circumstances and just life have changed that."

"That's sad, you know? I lost touch with all my school friends. Jeremy saw to that. I miss them." She wiped at a tear, angry with herself for that tear.

"Go ahead. Cry, sweetheart. Get mad. Yell at me. I'll find some rocks for you to kick." Barnabas gave a sad smile. "I can't imagine how your life was."

"I know. But God allowed it, didn't He? And I must accept that and then move on. I just don't want you hurt or any of the others hurt."

"It's a risk we take every day, sweetheart. We could get hurt in so many ways." He pulled into his parking spot at the building and shut off the truck

———

before he turned to her, reaching for her hands. "Let's pray, sweetheart. I feel the urge to bathe us in God's protection for the next few days."

"This is real, isn't it?" Aubrey bit at her lip. "I'm scared, love. I am so scared."

"And I am too. But we know that God will protect us. He will allow things to happen. That's part of life. We're not wrapped in cotton wool and put on a shelf. He expects us to continue going about our daily walk, trusting in Him."

"I know that, love. I know that in my heart. It's my head that I'm having trouble convincing of that." She blinked, a thought coming to her. "I don't get why Jason would be here, though. It should have been Jeremy."

"Jim said he saw an older man hanging around a vehicle near ours. He disappeared before Jim could approach him."

"That was likely Jeremy then. They're in town. Now what?"

"Now what? We continue. Buckley has asked if he and Locklin could have us for dinner tomorrow night. That came up late this afternoon. It's up to you."

"We need to, love. We can't continue to hide. Not at all." Aubrey drew a deep breath. "I'm going to be bold and you know that is not me. We need to go out and about. Go on the offensive, isn't that what they say?"

"It is. I'm just not sure if this is the right time."

———

"Barnabas!" Aubrey's voice held a note of shock. "I have lost ten years or so to him. I can't do this anymore."

"I know, sweetheart. How I know that! We need to make some plans. Dallas said he'd be around tomorrow, just as a friend, not an officer. Why don't we talk to him?"

"We can. Do you know anyone in security that you can talk with?"

"I do. A good friend. In fact, why don't I put Dallas off until Sunday? We can take off early in the morning and go see my friend. It's not that long a drive."

"We could do that?" Aubrey was still amazed at the freedom to live that she had once more.

"We can. If we leave early enough, we can stop at the Irish bakeshop for breakfast."

"Oh! I like that." She was out of the truck and running for the building before Barnabas could respond.

"Hey! Wait!" He ran after her, the locks on the truck clicking closed behind him.

She spun and then ran back towards him, feeling his arms hugging her tight. "I love you, Barnabas. Thank you." She reached up for his kiss.

Chapter 17

Her hand tight in Barnabas, Aubrey looked around the town of Riverville the next morning, surprise and then joy on her face. This is what I needed, Lord. To get away and do something for fun. Thank you.

Barnabas held the door to a bake shop open for her and they entered, Aubrey's eyes closing as she drew in a deep breath. The aroma of fresh baking and spices filled her senses. Her eyes popped open as she heard someone stop in front of them.

Dave Allison stood there, a grin on his face, even as he reached to shake Barnabas' hand.

"Barnabas! It's been a while. Good to see you! And who is this?" Dave's attention transferred to Aubrey.

"My bride, Dave. This is Aubrey. Aubrey, this is Dave, a friend. His wife runs this cafe with her grandmother and Dave's sister. Is Rylee around?"

"No, she's not in right yet. But what can I get you?"

"Whatever you want. I promised Aubrey breakfast here." Barnabas sat Aubrey at one of the tables and then approached the counter. "Dave? Is Abe around today?"

"He should be." Dave peered at the door. "In fact, there is Abe and Murphy."

Barnabas turned, then moved towards the two men who had just entered.

"Abe! Just the man I was looking for."

Abe Finlay looked around in surprise. "Barnabas Carey! You're in my town. That's a switch."

Murphy O'Brien reached to shake the other man's hand, a frown on his face. "You're looking ragged somewhat, Barnabas. Don't tell. You're in the middle of an adventure." He grinned.

Barnabas nodded even as he smiled. "I am. I ran away today with my bride, Aubrey. We're needing to pick your brains. I was hoping and praying that you'd be around."

Abe looked around, finding Aubrey watching them intently. "This is your bride?"

Barnabas reached out a hand to draw Aubrey to him. "This is Aubrey. It's a long story, but if you have time today, we'll run it by you and then see what suggestions that you can offer us."

"Aubrey, welcome to our town. It's good to finally meet the lady of this man's heart. Listen, how be we get what we came for? You bring your breakfast and then we'll head for Emma's business. She'll be anxious to meet you. She's been putting in some extra hours, not willingly, I might add, but necessary."

Aubrey stared around the reception area of the business Abe led them into, hearing his voice speaking with a lady in the back. She stopped in front of an enlarged picture of an eagle couple, drawing in her

—

breath. Murphy had been watching her and approached.

"Emma took that picture. She had been watching these eagles for years. She and Abe had been separated and kept apart for years. She told Jace, who works for her, that if she ever got that photo, then she knew what was unresolved in her life would be resolved. That was finding Abe once more."

"It's sad that they were kept apart. It's like Barnabas and me. I was kept imprisoned by someone who said that he was my guardian. Two years ago, he locked me into one room, cutting off all contact with Barnabas and everyone else. He's tracked me down to town. His son was in the diner we had dinner in last night. I need to know how to stay safe while trapping him. Is that too much to ask?"

"Not at all. Abe and I have a security team. His father started it. Abe took it over and then asked me to come into partnership with him. We have six other men on the team. Each of us has our specialties. We can meet and then come up with some ideas for you two. And if I know Emma, she'll want in on the search."

"She will? I'm sorry. I'm not sure that I understand." She looked past Murphy as Abe and a beautiful russet-haired lady approached.

"Aubrey, this is my wife, Emma. She's the one who has been helping out on the adventures your fellows have been on. At least some of them."

Emma simply hugged Aubrey and then drew her back to her office, seating her and then perching on the edge of the desk.

—

"Talk to me, Aubrey. I understand from Abe that you were imprisoned for a number of years. And that the man's son was watching you last night."

"I was. And Jason was." Aubrey explained it all to Emma, ending with a sigh. "What do I do, Emma? How do I stay safe, keep Barnabas safe, and not harm anyone else in the building?"

"That's a tough one. Abe will work with his team, come up with a plan, and then we'll come to see you. He'll need a day or so. Do you work?"

"No. I don't. I wish I could but it's not possible right now." Aubrey sighed, her eyes closing for a moment. "I had such dreams when I was at school. I took business courses, took courses in early childhood education. I wasn't sure quite what I had planned, but I wanted to work with children. Now, I'm not sure. Not seeing anyone for ten years other than just a few? That changes your perspective. A whole lot. I had time to read, what little he allowed me. I hid my Bible. He wanted it. Said it was full of lies and that I wasn't to read it. I memorized a lot too, just in case. I wasn't allowed a computer. A television. I had a phone but only limited access to it. There was an email that I refused to let him access."

"And you didn't ask for help?" Emma moved to sit beside her, hugging her.

Aubrey stared through blurred vision at the tears slashing off her hands. "I couldn't." Her voice was barely audible. "I couldn't. He had threatened to kill anyone who came to help me. I didn't want to be responsible for that."

—

"And that is part of how he kept control of you." Emma looked up as Barnabas appeared, on his knees beside Aubrey, wrapping her in his arms, and listened as he prayed for her.

"Barnabas? Do you have to head back today?" Abe spoke from the doorway.

"We do. Dallas is heading out late this afternoon to meet with us." Barnabas looked around.

"Then, we'll get what information that we can from you two. Murphy? Ready, I see." Abe grinned as a pen and pad of paper was shoved at him.

"Let's move to the reception area." Murphy stepped back that way. "I have beverages out here. Aubrey? Emma has some of that apple spice tea that I am told you like."

Chapter 18

Stretching out on the couch once they were home, Aubrey tucked one hand under the pillow her head was on, the other under her cheek. She smiled as she thought back over the day. Barnabas was still the fun man that she remembered, liking to tease and torment as her mother would have said, but with a steadiness and seriousness to him that she appreciated. It had always been there but was more enhanced now, she thought, reflective of what he did for a living and also what he had been through with his friends. A smile was still on her face as she drifted off to sleep, to sleep without dreams for once.

Barnabas pocketed his phone and turned from where he had stood, looking out the French doors in his home office. He sighed. He hadn't wanted to take that call but had no choice. John, one of the Foundation lawyers, had needed to speak with him. He had listened as well as Barnabas had brought him up to date on what they knew. John's wisdom of the years came through in the words and advice and the prayer that he offered.

Walking back through the apartment, he found it quiet, but not the silence that he had grown accustomed to over the years. He heard the soft instrumental music that Aubrey had turned on and smiled. He usually liked no music but knew that she needed this. He would not say no to her, not on something this minor, he thought. Barnabas stood for a moment, his eyes on his bride, before he moved forward on silent socked feet, to reach for the green, yellow and cream plaid velour blanket that she had found and bought for the living room. He covered her gently before dropping a kiss on her cheek, bringing a soft smile to her face.

Hearing a tap at the door, he headed that way, standing back as both Dallas and Breck entered. He frowned. It was only to be Dallas.

"Breck? You're here? Where's Neasa?"

"On her way. She knew that you two had been away today. She had been looking for Aubrey. She decided to make your supper, hoping that you hadn't eaten."

"We haven't. We've only been home for about thirty minutes or so. Coffee's on. I'll go wake Aubrey."

Dallas shook his head. "No, let her sleep. I can only imagine what poor sleep she has had over the years."

"That she has had. She's starting to talk more about what it was like. Middle of the night in the darkness talks. He was brutal with his words, Dallas. I don't know how she managed."

"God." Breck looked around before he set the mugs of coffee that he had filled on the table and pulled out a chair to sit. "Neasa hasn't said much but she did say that Aubrey told her that she spent a lot of time in prayer and memorization, just in case she lost her Bible."

"And he would have done that, wouldn't he?" Barnabas sent up a prayer for his bride, asking for healing and restoration for her. He looked at Dallas. "Dallas?"

"Barnabas?" Dallas grinned as he mimicked Barnabas. "I am here today as a friend. Nothing more. I have left the work and the case at the office, as they say. You need friends to come around you."

"I know I do, but I have one question. Jason?"

"Jason. Now that's an interesting man. He was arrested early today. Break and enter into the shelter. Cadee's father found him in the office and held onto him until the patrol officer arrived. He's not saying anything, but he had drugs, stolen jewelry, break and enter tools on his person. He's not able to make bail. No one is responding to his phone call."

"That is interesting." Barnabas looked around as he heard a tap on the door and then Neasa appeared, a basket in her hand. He rose and took it from her. "Supper, Neasa?"

"It is. If we put the oven on low, it will stay hot. I also have fixings for a tossed salad. Aubrey has expressed her desire to eat more of those."

"She has. Thank you." He hugged her before setting the casserole in the oven. "Tell me, Neasa. Has Aubrey said much?" He held up a hand. "I don't want you to break confidence with her. I just want to know that she is talking with someone, getting a female point of view."

"She is starting to, Barnabas. I have suggested that we contact Darcie and see what Darcie can offer."

"That's a good idea." Barnabas looked towards the doorway and then walked that way, finding Aubrey standing in the hallway, a confused look on her face. "Sweetheart?"

"Barnabas? Where is he? He's here, isn't he?" Aubrey spun in a circle before Barnabas swept her into his arms.

"No, he's not. Just Breck, Neasa, and Dallas. All here as friends." He frowned. "Did you hear him?"

"I thought I did. How would that be possible? I could hear him as plain as if he was standing right here."

Dallas had approached, a grim look on his face. "Let me search your apartment, Barnabas. Breck? Can we move the ladies and our meal to your place?"

"Absolutely." He was on his feet, helping Neasa gather the meal back up, turning off the oven, reaching for Aubrey's hand. "Here, Aubrey. Come with us." He nodded at Dallas as he swept the ladies out of the room.

Dallas grew even grimmer as he searched, finally turning to Barnabas.

"I need you out of here, friend. I have to bring in a team."

"He's been in here?"

"Someone has. Aubrey wasn't hearing things. If it had been different, then that would have been used against her. Knowing you and being here when she said it? That helps. I could search right away, without someone coming back in to remove what they had placed. I also asked for a locksmith to come out. Your locks are changed today."

Barnabas paled. "Okay. Whatever needs to be done. How do I tell her?"

"I'll be up as soon as the team gets here. I'll talk to you there. For now, you're just another one in danger, Barnabas. This time? You need to step back and let the rest of us work."

"I know. It's hard to do that."

"It is. Go on. Find Aubrey. I am praying for you both."

Chapter 19

Staring at Barnabas in horror, Aubrey felt his hands tighten on her shoulders. She knew Neasa and Breck were behind her, watching them closely. Her eyes closed as tears started, trickling down her face as she was unable to stop them. Barnabas gave an inaudible sound and simply swept her into his arms, holding her as tight as he could, his face pressed to her hair.

"He was in our apartment?" Her voice was low.

"He was, sweetheart. Or someone else was, setting up what Dallas found." He prayed for them, feeling her relax against him as he did so. *Lord, I could use some help. We need to live our lives, but he keeps interfering in them. How do we do this, Lord? How do I keep the love of my life safe?*

"What do we do, love?" Aubrey leaned back to look up at him. "What do we do? Do we stay there or move?"

"We can do that, even on a temporary basis. The apartment right next door is available. It might be best. That way, we're not on the main floor. Until this is solved." Barnabas looked up at a sound from Breck. "Breck?"

"You took the words out of my mouth, Barnabas. I was going to suggest that very thing. Dallas has the team in, you said?"

"He does. He didn't say how long they would be." Barnabas turned Aubrey around. "Aubrey, this has to be our decision, not mine. Not Dallas'. Not Breck's. It involves both of us."

Aubrey nodded, a sober look on her face. "I get that, Barnabas. Can we eat and then have a time of prayer? We need that, I think. Neasa has gone to all that work of preparing a meal." She moved away from him, towards the kitchen, Neasa following after stopping to hug Barnabas.

Breck motioned Barnabas back to his home office.

"What aren't you saying?"

Barnabas shrugged. "I really don't know. It's so puzzling. Dallas was heading to talk with the security team here." He blew out a breath, scrubbing at his face. "I wish I could just take her away until it was all over."

"And you can't. You mentioned that you had seen Abe?"

"I did. He had some ideas that I need to discuss with you and the other fellows. Can we set up a time on Monday, if we can do that? We need to keep Sunday as normal as possible, for all of us."

"It's already done. Buckley asked that we meet. Said he felt so burdened for you two, a that he wants to pull everyone in and work on this." Breck paused, his eyes studying his lifelong friend. "Barnabas? You have been there for each one of us. We have been friends pretty much all of our lives. We have had differences, but I don't remember us never being able to work through them or pray through them. This time? You're the one in need, the one who needs to be protected. Let us help you."

"It's humbling to have to say yes, but it is what it is, isn't it?" Barnabas sank down onto the couch, his head in his hands for a moment. "What can I say but thank you?"

"Nothing. It's what friends do. Let me pray with you right now." Breck prayed for Barnabas and Aubrey, Barnabas finding comfort in his prayer.

Mom is right. He has a powerful way of praying, of bringing a person right before God. We need to learn that. Not many of us do.

Neasa hesitated a moment, waiting until the men had lifted their heads before calling them to come and eat. Barnabas moved ahead of her to find Aubrey, while Neasa walked into Breck's hug, stifling a sob as she did so.

"Darling? What happened?"

Neasa shrugged. "It's so sad, Breck, what she was put through. How she had to live. She has a good attitude but I wonder what she was like before this."

"She was a lot of fun. A spitfire, Barnabas used to say. I see pieces of that, but this has changed her. It had to have. We'll pray for her, darling, and him. Let's eat. I know that we need to do that, even though not one of us feels much like it."

The meal was quiet, no one feeling much like talking. Barnabas looked around, sighed, and then began to speak, to talk about what Abe had told him.

—

Breck nodded. "He has more, doesn't he?"

Barnabas nodded. "He does. This is just what he and Murphy came up with. He'll speak to the others, talk to Doug and Caleb, he said. He threatened to send Eddy and Ben or even Frankie our way."

"Any one of those would be a help. The last three? They were or still are officers."

"That they are. I wouldn't mind talking to Eddie or Ben. Abe said to call them if I felt that I needed to."

"Probably a good idea." Breck rose as he heard a tap at the door and then stood back to let Dallas in. "Dallas? Sit. Have your dinner. Then we talk."

Dallas nodded, accepting with thanks the plate Neasa handed him. "I need this. It's been a long week. Neasa, your casseroles are always so delicious." He looked over at Barnabas and then Aubrey. "Let me eat. Then, we talk. And talk we will."

Chapter 20

Dallas finally shoved his plate away, a word of thanks as Breck rose to remove it, then sat back down. He eyed the other four at the table, his gaze stopping on Aubrey. She's calm, Lord, and I don't know how she can be. Not after what she heard. And we heard what she heard. He's a brute, Lord, and we need to stop him before he hurts either one of these two. And, dear Lord, I don't know that we can. He's so elusive.

"Dallas? What did you find?" Barnabas had an arm around Aubrey, feeling her leaning against him.

"Not what we wanted to. That's for certain. But what we expected." He looked at Aubrey. "I apologize. I should have swept the apartment but didn't think that there was a need, given the upped security. We are still determining how whoever it was got in. We have a suspicion on how. What did we find? Microphones. Some listening devices. A recorded message that was triggered at certain times of the day or night. How long have you felt that you were hearing something?"

"Just today. I haven't heard anything before tonight." She looked up at Barnabas. "I would have told you if I had."

"I know, sweetheart. Does that mean that they were in there today? They knew that we were away."

"I suspect that they had someone following you and when they found out that you would be away for a

—

while, moved in and set up their devices. We are confident that we have found all of them." Dallas stared down at the papers in front of him. "Barnabas. Aubrey. I can't begin to tell you how dangerous this has just gotten for both of you. They will be watching for each of you, either alone or together. Aubrey, I know that you like to walk around the gardens, and then around the building. All I can ask is that you have one of the security guards with you if Barnabas isn't. They're trained for this."

Aubrey shrugged. "I guess. It's not like when I was imprisoned, is it? At least, I have a choice as to what I do or don't do."

"That you do. Barnabas, now you. You move around a lot some days. Other days you are here. How much can you do with a conference or video calls?"

"Probably most of it. There are times when I do need to meet, to sign documents, etc. The board would come here. They have already said that. John said that he and the other lawyers would do the same. For now, some of what I do I can shift to Breck. He's offered to take up that."

"Good. Now, what did Abe have to say?"

"About what you said. He's meeting with his team and will send further advice. Emma has taken up the hunt, and I am sure that she'll soon be sending information and documents to you."

Dallas grinned. "She already is. Interesting fellow, this Jeremy. Aubrey, when I can sort through what she has sent, I want to meet with you and Barnabas. And I spoke with John earlier about what he has. He is sure that Jeremy will try to have you committed under a mental health assessment. John's already working on that. Darcie Foster will be in touch with you either tomorrow or Monday. Talk with her. She's a resource that is used, not as much as we would like to, but she is very picky about how much she does that now. And it is usually just for friends or their family."

"She does?" Aubrey was hesitant to agree. "But why would she want to speak with me? Who is she?"

"She has an arts and crafts store and sells it online as well. She is well respected among artisans in her area. But she was a forensics psychologist who was treated poorly by the law officer she was employed by and withdrew from the force. She has kept up her credentials, which is good. We have used her with a couple of the ladies here. Neasa was one."

Aubrey's attention turned to Neasa, to find her nodding.

"She did. She provided expert witness documentation as well as a profile on who was after me. She nailed him. Darcie will work with you, Aubrey. She will not come across in a threatening manner. I found her very calming, in fact."

Breck nodded. "She is that and more, Aubrey. She and her husband, Doug, had a horrible experience with someone on the force targeting different towns and emergency personnel. He almost killed her."

Aubrey's eyes had been steady on Breck. "So, she knows what it is like? Then, I do want to speak to her. Her experience is of course different from mine, but I feel that I need to talk with someone, someone with training, and someone who can understand."

"We'll make sure that happens, sweetheart." Barnabas tightened his arm on her. "For now, let's set all this aside. We need to spend hours in prayer. We don't have that tonight, but we can spend time with our friends, finding the peace and wisdom that we need to go forward."

Chapter 21

Late that night, Aubrey stood in Barnabas' office, looking around, feeling very uncomfortable. He watched her before he approached her.

"You okay?"

"No. No, I'm not. I hate that someone was in here." She looked up at him as she stood in the circle of his arms. "I can't sleep, Barnabas. I can't even think about living here right now. But that's not fair to you."

"No, it's not fair to you. This is your home, one that someone has walked into. Let me pack up some stuff for us. We can move up to the one beside Breck. It's all ready for that."

"Do you think we should?"

"I do." He hugged her tight. "If that brings peace to you, then we do. We take what we need for tonight and tomorrow morning. Then, we come back down, take up what we need for the week and go from there."

"Okay. I'm sorry."

"There's nothing that you need to apologize for. You didn't invite them in, now did you? They made the decision to invade our home. We will step back from it, assess how we feel after a few days. If it means that we move to another one, then we do. We do what is best for you and what is best for us as a couple."

Aubrey stood on her tiptoes, reaching to kiss him. "Thank you, Barnabas. You are not downplaying my concerns or belittling me. I can't tell you how many times Jeremy did that."

"No, I won't. I may have to act suddenly if you are in danger, but if I can discuss it with you, then I will. Come on, sweetheart. Let's grab some of our things and head on upstairs."

Aubrey settled down to sleep, not knowing that Barnabas had settled down in the living room, his Bible open on his knee, but his heart raised in prayer. This was the dangerous time, he thought, with their enemy hitting in spurts. They never knew when he would. It would be wearing on them as individuals but also as a couple. Lord, we need to be connected and together. We are just young in our marriage and already facing what many couples never do. My friends here know what it is like to some extent. But, Lord, we need to rely on You. Teach us how to do that. Please, dear Lord, protect my Aubrey? Keep her from harm. And keep me from harm, dear Lord, so that I can protect her.

Aubrey rose in the night, looking for Barnabas, pausing in the living room doorway, a smile on her face. Barnabas had fallen asleep on the couch, his head resting on the back of it. She simply moved to snuggle up against him, setting his Bible to a table and spreading the blanket that she had wrapped herself in over them. She slept as well, not realizing the danger that would start hitting at them that week, harder and harder, and putting both their lives in danger.

—

Barnabas rose the next morning, stretching, a frown on his face before he shook his head. Fell asleep on the couch and Aubrey came to find him. He smiled as he watched her sleep before he headed for a shower and shave and then to the kitchen to make his coffee.

Another Sunday, Lord. Another week. And this week? I am not eager to start it at all. I fear for what is coming. I have this sense of doom and gloom, as Mom would say, hanging over us. Please, Lord? Go before us. Protect us. If we are hurt, heal us. That's all that I can ask, isn't it? Except to say thank you. Dear Lord, You are right here and I need to remember that.

A few hours later, Barnabas stood at the back of the church, watching Aubrey as she was surrounded by the ladies of the building, Hagen's young son in her arms. He had taken one look at her and launched himself into her arms, hugging her tightly and then covering her face with sloppy kisses. He refused to return to his mother, his head tucked under Aubrey's chin, thumb in his mouth as he grinned at his mother. Aubrey just stood and rocked slightly, a hand rubbing at his back.

Breck stood beside him, eyes watchful, knowing that the other men in the building were doing the same, on the lookout for someone out of character.

"Did you decide what you are doing?"

"About the apartment? For now, we'll move out for a week. Aubrey's not happy with that. She hates being chased from her home."

"And I can understand that. After not having a home for all those years? Being caged like she was? I

---

can almost guarantee you that she'll change her mind and refuse to leave the apartment. I spoke with security this morning. They're working on upping what they need to on your apartment. They have asked that you not use the French doors in the living room or the office for now."

Barnabas nodded, having already reached that conclusion. He had been watching Aubrey closely that morning.

"I agree. I suspect that we won't be moving. We can agree to not use the doors. That's not an issue. How strong a lock are they putting on them?"

"Not so much a lock as stronger sensors. That way, if you or she needs to escape through either one, you can." Breck reached for Neasa's hand. "Call me, Barnabas. We need to talk about relieving some of your duties. You're stretching yourself thin and have been for a while. Your Dad knows that. I would not be surprised to hear that he is talking with the other board members."

"He is. He already spoke to me. He wants to shift some things to you, more of the acquisitions line. That's what you already do. And some of the investigations into new missionaries." Barnabas paused. "He did say that they were setting up a new position and had already spoken with someone. Dallas would be good to come on board, but I am not sure that he's ready to leave this force."

"He's ready." Neasa spoke up. "He's more than ready, Barnabas. He did say that he was looking into something, but hasn't said much more."

"He did? Now we know how to pray for him better." Barnabas tucked Aubrey under his arm as she approached him. "Where's Heath?"

She laughed. "His father finally claimed him. Hannah wasn't happy that she couldn't come to me. I need to go visit them tomorrow." Her face was aglow from the love the little ones had shown her.

"Sounds like a plan. Come one, sweetheart. Mom and Dad would like us to come for dinner if you want."

"I want. Your mother is such a special lady. She did well raising her son."

"She did, did she?" Barnabas shot a look around before he kissed her. "Then, let's go find them. And we do need to discuss where we're living. I don't think you want to move."

"No. I don't." Aubrey shook her head. "He would win again if we leave. Breck said that we can't use the French doors, at security request. I can live with that. Can you?"

"I can. I talked to him too. Let's go, sweetheart." He tucked her into his truck and stood, looking around. Someone is out there, aren't they, Lord? Protect my lady, that's all I ask.

Chapter 22

The next day, Aubrey packed up what they had taken to the other apartment, ready to move back downstairs. She wandered the apartment, tidying it, cleaning as needed even though she had been told the cleaners would be through to do that. She was making work, she knew, feeling impending doom handing over her like a storm-darkened rain cloud.

Sighing, Aubrey picked up the bag that she had set by the front door and moved out of it, locking it behind her. She walked down the flight of stairs, heading for the second flight before her footsteps slowed. Fear coursed through her.

"Jason? How did you get in here? This is a private building."

Jason sneered at her. "That's what you think. There are ways to get in." He walked towards her even as she backed away from him. "You're coming with me. You don't have a choice."

"I don't think so." Aubrey felt for the stair railing, hoping that she could make it down the stairs and to the security guard before Jason could reach her. "This is my home."

Jason sneered as he laughed, a cruel, menacing laugh. "Nope. You're coming with me. We're leaving this town. Dad promised that you would be mine."

"He did?" Aubrey's brow grew dark. "Sorry. Not happening." She threw the bag that she was carrying towards him and turn, almost falling, as she took the steps at a run, her breath catching in a sob.

Jason dodged the bag and sprang after her, catching an arm and pulling her with him as he tried to descend the steps. Aubrey's hand clung to the railing even as she struggled to free her other one, the one that he was twisted viciously in his determination to move her down the stairs and away from help.

Her hand slipped from the railing and Aubrey flew forward, her body slamming into Jason as he pulled her towards them. This sent the pair off balance and they tumbled down the stairs, Aubrey's scream ringing through the lobby. They lay in a crumpled heap until Jason staggered to his feet, disoriented. He looked around and then grabbed Aubrey's wrist, dragging her unconscious body across the dark hardwood floor of the lobby, muttering to himself that she was his and no one else.

Branigan and Bradon had heard Aubrey's scream, took a look at one another and then were flying from the conference room, Bradon's dog, Kade, forging ahead. He shot a look back at his master who ordered him to take down the man. A threatening growl erupted from Kade's throat and his toes dug into the floor as he surged ahead, his jaws clamping down firmly on Jason's arm. The force of the dog's body hitting him took Jason to the floor, even as Bradon ordered Kade to release and stand guard. Kade stood back, a growl coming from him even as Jason tried to crawl away, Kade circling around him to keep him from doing just that.

Branigan and Bradon were on their knees beside Aubrey, feeling for a pulse, their faces holding shock before they darkened with anger. Bradon's phone was out as he called for help.

"Where's Paul? I thought that he was on duty." Branigan looked around before he was on his feet, heading for the security desk. "He's here. He's out cold." Branigan stood back up, before he walked towards Jason, his booted feet preventing the man from crawling forward. "What did you do to them?"

"She's mine. I'm taking her with me." Jason lay still, even as the sirens sounded and red and blue emergency lights flashed in the parking lot.

Branigan didn't move, even when the patrol officers poured into the lobby. He heard a sound and turned.

"Brady? Good. I was praying it would be you."

"What happened, Branigan?"

"We don't know. We found them like this. He was dragging Aubrey towards the door. She has not moved."

"Okay. Patrick?" Brady turned to his partner who was already on his knees beside Aubrey.

"Backboard, I think, Brady. And collar. I wonder if she fell down the stairs." Patrick shot a look towards them.

"That's possible. Barnabas mentioned this morning when I saw him that they were coming back down to the first floor."

Bradon stood near them, his hand on Kade's head. "More than likely, Brady. There's a bag of Barnabas' on the floor at the foot there."

The two paramedics worked quickly, assessing Aubrey before shifting her to the backboard, neck collar in place. They moved through the lobby, heading for the paramedic rig, whoever lived in the building and were there, standing watching, horror, concern, and then anger showing on their faces. Buckley and Locklin headed for their vehicle, intent on being there for Barnabas. Locklin's phone was out before she paused.

"Where is Barnabas today?"

"Andy flew him up north for some meetings. He said he'd be back late this afternoon." Buckley sighed. "Call Bruce. See if he and Elizabeth can come. I didn't see them there."

"No, they weren't. I hate this, Buckley. I just pray that she's not hurt too badly."

"As am I." Buckley parked at the hospital and then was out of the truck, reaching for Locklin's hand as they ran for the Emergency Department.

Doc looked around as he heard Brady's voice before he moved towards him, a frown on his face.

"Brady?"

"It's Aubrey, Doc. We think that she took a tumble down the stairs at the building, but we're not sure. She hasn't been awake since we got there."

Doc shot him a look before pointing to an empty room. "For once, I have a room that I can put her in. They've been hard to come by today." His stethoscope was in his hands as he listened to Brady's report. "Okay. Barnabas?"

"Not there. I'm not sure where he is today." Brady had helped to shift Aubrey to the stretcher in the examining room. "I'm off, Doc. I'll be back." He took a look at Aubrey before he shook his head, finding Patrick waiting outside for him.

"Brady? What happened?"

"I have no idea. Branigan said that Barnabas had told him that they were moving back down to his own apartment after it was searched. This is frustrating, Patrick. We don't know who or why."

"And I'll talk to our supervisor. You'll be pulled back in to help." Patrick slammed the back door of the rig before he stood, his fingers rubbing together. "Barnabas?"

"Not sure. Buckley was following us, so he'll track him down. I imagine that he'll have already called Bruce and Elizabeth."

"I'm sure. Let's hit the road, pal. It's going to be a long day."

Chapter 23

Andy, the Foundation pilot, watched as Barnabas ran towards him, his briefcase swinging beside him. He followed Barnabas up the stairs to the plane, pulling them in and locking it.

"All set?"

"I am, Andy. It's been a long day. Thanks for sticking around."

Andy grinned. "It's not like I was going anywhere. But you are welcome. Buckle up and we'll be home in an hour or two."

His briefcase tucked away, Barnabas sat back into his seat, his head on the headrest, his eyes closing as fatigue weighed them down. He was tired, he thought, but today had been necessary. He would be back in time to meet with the men, finding out what all they had discovered, and he was sure that they had discovered facts and people. Aubrey needed to be there, he thought. He slept, weary from the last six weeks or so.

Andy landed the plane, did his post-flight check, and then stood, watching as Breck walked towards him, Neasa standing by Breck's truck.

"Breck? You're here?"

"I am. Barnabas?"

"He was still asleep. I was heading up to wake him. Something's wrong?"

"There is. Barnabas, you're on your feet." Breck looked towards his friend as he descended the stairs.

"I am. But you're here." Barnabas frowned.

"I am. I need you to come with me. We'll get your truck later." Breck's hand on his arm stopped Barnabas in his tracks.

Barnabas stared at his friend. "Aubrey? Is she okay?"

"No, she's not." Breck's hand tightened on the arm. "She was hurt this morning, Barnabas. She's in hospital. Your parents are with her."

"How?" When Breck didn't respond, Barnabas spoke again. "How? Tell me, Breck, how was she hurt."

"Jason made his way into the building. He took down Paul. And then searched for Aubrey. We think that he found her and that she was trying to escape him. We found one of your duffle bags on the main floor. What we think happened is that she fell down the stairs to the lobby." Breck paused, unable to continue for a moment. "Bradon and Branigan heard her scream and ran for there. They found Jason dragging her body across the floor, intent on taking her with him. Kade took him down."

"How bad?"

"I don't know. Doc was on duty. Brady and Patrick were the paramedics who responded. Come on, my friend. Into my truck. We'll get you to your lady."

Barnabas paced the Emergency Department waiting room, a short time later, dodging the people moving around, the little children who were tired and cranky and just wanted to go home, the security guards who walked among them. He knew his friends were there. He had greeted each one of the men, being told that the ladies had gathered in the chapel. Bruce had stood waiting for him, just enveloping his son into his arms, feeling the shudders of fear running through his son's body.

"Dad?"

"No word, yet, son. We've been back. Apparently, we're listed after you are." He turned his son to the door, an arm across his shoulders. "In we go. Mom is here. She refused to go with the ladies, said that she had to be here for you."

Elizabeth held her son, feeling the sobs that he refused to release shaking him. She prayed for her son, a man grown and married, but still needing his mother at a time like this. She finally drew him to a chair.

"Mom?"

"I was back just now, son. She's still unconscious. Doc said that they were waiting on some imaging results before he would know more. Breck called us as the plane landed and we got word to Doc."

Doc looked around from where he sat at a computer, his reading glasses on his nose, as a nurse approached.

"Barnabas is here."

"He is? Thanks, Stacy. Now, the results are back?"

"We have everything, Doc. The imaging, blood work, anything that you asked for." Stacy paused. "Do you want me to find him?"

Doc stood, a sigh coming from him. It had been a hectic, overly busy day. Having Aubrey arrive as she did had not eased a burden from him.

"No. I'll go find him. Thanks. There's a room available on the medical floor?"

"There is. A private room came up. We'll move her upstairs now if you want."

"Please. I'll find him and bring him upstairs." Doc stopped in his tracks, a prayer raising for both Barnabas and Aubrey. She's a fortunate lady, isn't she, Lord? It could have been so much worse, but she's not out of the woods, not by a long shot. Heal her, please, dear Lord?

Chapter 24

Doc paused once more outside the doors to the Emergency Department rooms, his eyes on Barnabas as he paced, Breck at his side. Those two young men? They have been friends for so long. Together in trouble, what little they got into, together in fun, standing shoulder to shoulder with one another. Barnabas was there for Breck with Neasa and now Breck was there for Barnabas. Their friendship is changing and evolving, like it will as they live life, Doc thought.

Barnabas turned towards Doc and then moved to him, his parents at his side, Breck stepping back and reaching for Neasa's hand as he watched. Breck prayed for his friend, not sure how to pray.

"Doc? Aubrey?" Barnabas had trouble even speaking, his fear that great.

"We're moving her upstairs right now to a bed on the medical floor. Come on. I just finished my shift and am heading that way, to sign her off to the physician there. Bruce, Elizabeth?"

"We're coming, whether you allow it or not, Doc." Elizabeth's arm was around her son. "We're not deserting these two."

"Didn't think you would." Doc remained quiet until he stood outside the room where Aubrey lay. "Let me talk with her new physician and then I'll be right back."

Doc was as good as his word, back in no time to beckon the three to the waiting room, finding it empty.

"Sit. Barnabas? I'll let you go in but first, we need to talk."

Barnabas sat as requested, his parents on either side of him, Bruce's arm around his shoulders, his mother's hands on his.

"Doc? What aren't you saying?"

Doc nodded. Right to the point, as always.

"I can't tell you what happened. That's not my place. Besides, I don't have that information. The patrol officer who came in with her was heading out to speak with Dallas. Dallas has been by and will be by later, he said." Doc hesitated for a moment, bringing fear to Barnabas' face. "As to her injuries? She has a concussion. Multiple bruising and bumps. It is the spine that we have been concerned about."

"Her spine? Please, Lord, not that!" Barnabas buried his face into his hands.

"Right now, son, there is some swelling around the lower spine. There doesn't appear to be any injury, but she has limited response and movement in her lower extremities. We need to keep her here and still until the swelling can go down. How long that will take, I don't know."

"Will she walk?" Barnabas searched his friend's face.

———

"I don't see why not, but she will need to take care. No stairs at all. If she has to be in a wheelchair for the first while, that is what will be recommended."

"We're on the first floor, so that works. And we have the elevator." Barnabas' mind had started to race. "Special bed or anything like that?"

"Not yet. We'll see how she does. I expect her to be here for at least a week. Dallas has said that he is arranged for security to take over here from his officer and they will be here all day and all night as long as she is here."

"Did he say who? Do I know them?"

Doc grinned before he sobered. "Oh, I think you do. It's Abe and his men. And he has indicated that if he needs to, he has friends who will gladly step in and take over."

"Oh, that's good. Dad, apartments?"

"Done already, son. Dallas approached me not long before you came in." Bruce's arm tightened around his son's shoulders. "Let us pray with you, son, and then Doc will take you to your lady."

Barnabas finally stood in the doorway to the room where his bride lay, sorrow in his heart that she had been hurt and that he had not been there to protect her. He walked forward on quiet feet, a prayer rising, before he stood, his eyes on the medical equipment surrounding her. He studied that and then dropped his vision to Aubrey.

"Oh, Aubrey! Sweetheart! I'm so sorry. So, so sorry. I didn't want you hurt and he came after you when I wasn't there to protect you. Please? Forgive me." He laid a gentle hand against her face, finding her skin cold and damp, before he reached for a hand, holding it, finding her fingers limp against it. Lord, please? Please heal my lady? I don't know that I can go on without her.

Sobs rose once more within him. This time, he didn't try to control them. Tears flowed down his face, dropping to the pillow as he laid his head beside her, a kiss on her cheek. Lord? Why? I don't understand it. Why Jason? Where was Jeremy?

Chapter 25

Two days had gone by since the accident. Aubrey was still sedated, letting her body heal, the physicians watching the swelling around her spine. Barnabas had refused to leave her, telling Breck to search for what needed to be done in the office and take care of it, if he would. Bruce had disappeared with Breck to do just that, the two men working to clear off as much as they could. The board had moved in as well, doing what they could to help, knowing that Barnabas would not leave his bride. And it was as it should be, they decided among themselves. It was nearing the holidays, anyway, Bruce had stated. They would soon be taking the time to spend with their families and what could be put off to the new year, would be.

Aubrey's eyes flickered late that afternoon, as she roused slightly. Barnabas was on his feet, his hand resting against her face, the other hand holding hers tightly, feeling her fingers tighten on his.

"Sweetheart? Can you hear me? Come on, sweetheart. Open your beautiful eyes." Barnabas knew that he was pleading but that was all he could do. He could not take her place, as much as he wanted to.

"Barnabas? Where am I?" Aubrey spoke without opening her eyes, her tongue licking at her dry lips.

"You had an accident, sweetheart. You're in the hospital."

"Take me home, please? I can't do this." Aubrey slept without knowing that tears of pain were trickling down her face, breaking Barnabas' heart.

"I will, sweetheart, just as soon as I can." He reached out to wipe away the tears, knowing that God was healing her, but just how much before she went home, no one knew.

Bruce stood for a moment watching his son, praying for the younger couple, before he walked forward. His arm around his son, he prayed for them before he directed Barnabas from the room, nodding at Murphy who stood at the door. He knew others of Abe's men were around.

"Sit, son." He handed him the takeout cup of coffee that he had left in the care of Imly, who had approached him earlier that day worried about Barnabas.

"Dad? I thought you had a meeting today."

"I did. Breck is sitting in for me. It's the last one before the holidays."

"It is? I thought we had a number scheduled for next week."

"The board has met. We have put off anything that we can until the new year. It is only right. They want your mother and me to spend the time with you and Aubrey." He nodded towards the room. "How is she?"

"She roused enough to recognize me. She wants me to take her home. And I can't do that."

"No, not yet. What have the physicians said?"

———

"The swelling is down a bit but not where it can be for her to leave. It wasn't supposed to be like this, Dad."

"I know, son. I know that." Bruce sighed, sitting back and sipping at his coffee. "We never told you that your mother had an accident before you were born. She had some spinal damage, not a lot, but enough that some of the nerves to her right leg were damaged."

"She did? Is that why she limps sometimes?"

"It is. Arthritis has also set into that hip."

"I wish I had known, Dad. She did things for me when I was young that she shouldn't have."

"Your mother has never asked or wanted to be pampered. If she did things for you, it was because she wanted to. She didn't want her injury to play a part in your life." Bruce sipped at his coffee again. "What has Dallas said?"

"I haven't talked to him since the day it happened. He hasn't been around." Barnabas pulled out his phone. "Oh, a text message. He's heading this way. Wants to know that I have security tight to me."

"And you do. Murphy is on the door. That Luke and Joseph are around here, somewhere. They are working in shifts, Abe rotating around as he needs to. He also has other friends moving in to help."

"He does? Who?"

"Men by the name of Eddie, Ben, Frankie, Doug, Dave, Gideon." Bruce shook his head. "All of the younger men have been involved in adventures as he terms it. Eddie is his uncle. Ben a good friend who is a retired officer."

"I will owe so much when this is over."

"Not at all." Abe sat down beside Barnabas. "You have provided so much over the years, Barnabas. I don't think you understand how you have been a source of encouragement to others. You live your name, every day." Abe nodded towards Bruce. "How's Aubrey?"

"She was awake, sort of. Asked me to take her home." Barnabas grew tense for a moment. "I don't know how to do this. I really don't."

"One day at a time, Barnabas. One day at a time. That's how Emma and I did it when we were separated by her aunt's third husband. She thought I was dead. I thought she didn't want anything to do with me. We reunited and are stronger as a couple." Abe looked pensive. "If you ask any of my men, my friends, they will tell you the same. That what they went through brought that to them. God protected all of them, even when they were at the point of death. The same as your friends. My sister, Rebecca? Her first husband was killed when they had been married for three months. Gideon was from our town, had left and then returned. He was able to step in and protect her."

"I see that you have interesting friends as well." Bruce watched his son closely. "Now, Abe? You said you had your security expert going over our building."

"I have. He is impressed with whoever it is that did your security system. He has talked to the head of security there, made a few minor suggestions regarding access and in particular, Barnabas' suite."

"Thanks, Abe." Barnabas was on his feet, moving towards Aubrey, his steps slow as fatigue hit him. Murphy watched him, a hand out to help him as he paused at the door before he nodded and entered the room, the door swishing closed behind him.

Chapter 26

Four days later, Aubrey frowned past the physiotherapist who stood at the side of the bed, frustrated that Aubrey refused to look at her.

"Aubrey, we need to do this. You have to be able to walk to leave."

"Says who? That's not what I was told. Please? Leave?" Aubrey watched her walk away before her head went back on the pillow. Forgive me, Lord? I am just so tired, hurting, and uncertain of anything any more.

Cadee and Jaxcy watched for a moment before they approached her. The ladies of the building, including Anna, had been coming in twos to visit her, spacing them out so they didn't tire her out.

"Aubrey? Rebelling?" Jaxcy grinned at her as Aubrey raised her head. "Not wanting to do the exercises?"

"No. I know why they want that, but I just can't. Not here. I need to go. I feel like I am still Jeremy's prisoner." Aubrey studied the two women, seeing them nod.

"That's what we thought. Here. Let us help you up. Cadee has some clothes for you. Barnabas is speaking with the physician. He's taking you home today, he says."

"He is? He didn't tell me." Aubrey accepted Cadee's help to dress.

"He was watching when the physiotherapist walked in. He knows how you feel without you saying anything. Here. We have a wheelchair for you. What do you want to take with you?"

"Just the flowers, I guess. There are so many."

"Then, pick what you want and we'll take off the cards and let the nurses distribute them."

"No, that's not right."

"It is. There are some here who have no one who visits them, receive no flowers. These will be a source of encouragement and pleasure to them." Jaxcy was working away as she spoke, pulling off the cards and tucking them into a pocket.

"Wow! You know, I never thought of it that way." Aubrey looked up. "Does the Foundation have a ministry that does that? Provides flowers and what not to those in the hospital or retirement homes?"

"Not that I am aware of. There you go. That can be your ministry." Cadee grinned at her, looking around as Barnabas appeared. "Barnabas, Aubrey just came up with her own ministry."

"She did?" He crouched down beside the wheelchair. "Ready to leave?"

"I am. The ministry? Jaxcy and Cadee suggested that I leave the flowers here and let the nurses distribute them. Does the Foundation do that for the ones who don't have anyone?"

Barnabas shook his head. "No, they don't. I'm not sure if we have discussed it. But we will. You're volunteering?"

"I am, I guess. I know what it's like to be alone. To not live life as it is meant to be." Aubrey watched him, seeing how he was processing her words. "Not right now, of course. And not without approval."

"We'll look into that in the new year. Right now, you need to be home." He stood, his hands on the handles of the wheelchair before he prayed for her, for himself, and for his friends.

Nathaniel watched as they walked towards him, a grin on his face.

"Blowing the joint, Aubrey?"

She laughed. Each of Abe's men had walked in and introduced themselves, endearing themselves to her. "I am. Thankfully. That means you get to go home."

"Oh, we will. Once we're satisfied that you're okay and settled, we'll hit the road. Ben and Marg and Eddie and his Peggy are staying put for now. They like the building and the area."

"They are?" Barnabas was surprised. "That's good, I guess."

"It is. They are a wealth of information, Barnabas. Talk to them."

"We will." He gently scooped Aubrey up and set her on the seat, reaching to pull her seatbelt over her to snap it shut. He studied her and then reached to kiss her, her hand resting on his shoulder. "I love you, sweetheart."

"I love you. But can we leave? I feel someone watching us."

"And there is. Jason isn't out. He hasn't been able to make his bail. Jeremy has been seen around."

"Will he haunt me forever? How do we catch him?"

Chapter 27

Late that night Barnabas walked the apartment, his mind working overtime as he thought about what had happened. He sighed. He was no further ahead, he decided, then he had been, other than more worried about his bride. He turned and walked towards the bedroom, a frown on his face as he didn't find her. Hearing muttering, he headed for the kitchen, pausing in the doorway, a smile crossing his face.

Aubrey had decided that she was hungry and needed her apple spice tea. Only she couldn't find it.

"Lose something?"

"I did. My tea. It's not where I left it."

Barnabas froze. "It's not? I didn't move it." He gently moved her back from the cupboard and to a chair at the table. "Let me have a look." He searched, finding it in the wrong cupboard. "This is not right." He spun, heading for the lobby, finding Murphy and Ian there. "Fellows? Can you come to our apartment? We just found Aubrey's tea out of place. I don't know that the cupboards were searched, but if they were, the team would not have moved anything from cupboard to cupboard."

The two men were on their feet, heading after Barnabas, frowns on their faces. This is what they had expected, Ian thought. It wasn't just that things were placed, but that things were moved.

"Okay. Where should it be?" Murphy nodded as Aubrey pointed to the cupboard over the coffeemaker.

"I always keep it there. The kettle is underneath. I don't get why it would be in another cupboard."

"Because someone has moved it and moved it for a reason. Did either one of you touch it?" Ian looked at them as they looked at one another and then shook their heads. "Can you call that friend of yours? I need to know if they searched the cupboards and moved anything. And he needs to get out here. This is something that we have seen before."

Barnabas nodded, making the call to Dallas. "He was on his way out, he said. Now what?"

"Now what is that you and Aubrey move from this room and into another room. Or even another apartment."

"Not again!" Aubrey's voice was almost a sob. "I thought it was safe."

"And it should be. We just need to go through everything again, just to see if anything has been tampered with."

Aubrey paled. "Tampered with? As in poison?"

Murphy nodded as he crouched down beside her, an arm resting on the table. "Or an explosive or something corrosive. One of our ladies couldn't get her phone to shut off. It triggered an explosion. So, you see, we need to ensure that nothing like that is here."

Barnabas drew her up and away, exchanging a look with Murphy as he stood. "Our fellows will be working on this full time now. If you need to speak with any of them, the conference room is where you'll find them."

"Abe said he would tomorrow. I need to let him know about this." Murphy's phone was out.

Breck paused in the hallway, having come to see what he could do for the couple.

"Barnabas?"

Barnabas sighed, his arm around Aubrey. "Her tea was moved from cupboard to cupboard. Dallas is on his way out. Can we come to visit you and Neasa? I want Aubrey somewhere she can rest."

"Sure. Neasa was concerned enough that she sent me down." Breck watched as Barnabas scooped Aubrey into his arms. "What can I bring for you?"

"Her pain medications. The anti-inflammatories. They're on the counter in the bathroom. I just put them there." Barnabas sighed once more. "I'll head for the elevator."

Murphy watched them walk away before he turned to Breck. "Her medications? They're safe?"

"They should be. I had them filled at our regular pharmacy." He paled. "You don't think?"

"I do."

"Then, let me talk to Doc. He might have something here that we can use." Breck was away, hating to disturb Doc, but knowing the man well enough that he would be willing to do what he needed to.

Neasa turned from the spare bedroom where she had turned down the blankets for Aubrey, praying for her friend. She doesn't need this, Lord, not when she's hurting so badly. She walked out of the room, into Breck's arms.

"Breck?"

"I gave Barnabas the medications from Doc. He's talking with Dallas right now. What can we do for her?"

"Right now? She's not even sure herself what she wants or needs, other than her husband. I promised her a cup of tea."

"Okay. Let's do that. Some toast or crackers?"

Neasa nodded, reaching for a tray. "I think so. She's nauseous, she said. Crackers will work." She paused, her eyes on the ceiling as she tried to control her own tears. Breck just wrapped her into his arms.

"We'll help all we can. She's independent, not wanting to be a burden. She also doesn't want to be locked away somewhere, and that's a possibility."

"I know." Neasa whispered her response. "I hate this for her. She's had one-third of her life taken away from or almost that. How close are you to finding him?"

"Not close enough. We need to talk to her again, to pick her brain to find out what else that she can tell us."

"Let me or one of the ladies do that. She might open up more to one of us."

Chapter 28

Barnabas wandered the conference room the next morning, a mug of coffee in his hand that he sipped from once in a while. He was on his own, it was that early. The fact of the matter was he had not slept. He had held Aubrey all night as she slept, her body twitching and twisting, the pain medications not working. To say that he was worried was an understatement. All he could do was pray for his bride.

Reading the whiteboards as he stopped at each one, Barnabas nodded. They are finding more and more information, aren't they, Lord? I see Emma's hand in some of it. Thank you for such a friend as she is. He turned as he heard the door open and close and footsteps approaching him.

Burnie stood watching his friend. How do we do this, Lord? How do we encourage him? And Aubrey? She has to be hurting, and he's hurting because she is.

"Burnie?"

"Barnabas? I see you're here bright and early. I thought that I would be the first one."

"Not today." Barnabas rubbed at his burning eyes, lack of sleep exacerbating that. "You fellows have been busy."

"We have. Breck pulled us all back from work. He talked to each one of our employers, you know."

"I suspected that he would. He's done it in the past."

"But not for you. They're concerned, my friend. Your encouragement over the years, not just in finding us to work for them, but in other ways? They want to repay it, but they're not sure how. The word on the street is that they are looking for Jeremy and whoever it is that he has employed. The Foundation has done too much down there for the people not to help."

"I'm sure that they're looking. He's likely coming back and forth, not wanting to stay around. Not just yet."

Blair spoke from his other side, coming in and just standing beside him. "Paul said that they've found signs of someone watching the building. Not enough that they can get a sense other than it's a female."

"Female? That's different. It's usually the men who are watching us."

"Jeremy's a different foe than we have faced. We still don't have a sense of why."

"Why? Aubrey?" Barnabas turned as he heard other footsteps and found all the men there. "That's what's puzzling us. She can't give a reason, other than he wanted her to take up a musical career. Jason told her that she had been promised to him. She doesn't understand that, either. Jeremy was careful, she said, to limit her exposure to him."

"That is weird." Benen pulled out the chair he usually sat in. "What would cause him to say that?"

"Revenge, maybe." Baird sat as well, booting up his computer. "I've come across some news articles about him. He's tried that before with other ladies. They've had to take out restraining orders against him."

"He has?" This from Brennen. "Has he been able to make bail?"

"No. Not that I know of." Barnabas turned back to a whiteboard. "Logic problem again? How is that working?"

"Not so well this time. We only have Jeremy and Jason. That's not enough." Buckley stood beside him this time. "How be we break off and pray and then get to work?"

Barnabas nodded, his eyes on his friends before he approached Brady. "Brady? Pray with me today?"

"I was going to ask you the same thing."

Barnabas finally sat back, watching and listening as the men bounced ideas from one to the other. They work well as a team, the adventures they all underwent concreting that, he thought. He sighed to himself. Lord, how do we do this? How do we find Jeremy? And now this woman? Who is she? Why watch us? He sat upright before he rose and headed for the whiteboard, Brandon following him.

"You had a thought."

"I did. This female who has been watching us. Whose side is she on?"

Brandon stared at him. "Whose side? Jeremy's?"

"But what if there is someone else? Someone behind Jeremy?" Barnabas staggered for a moment, Brandon's hand going out to steady him. "I just had a horrible thought. What if it hasn't been Aubrey? That she was hidden away, to get to me, and through me to the Foundation?"

Chapter 29

The men's heads all raised abruptly from their work, their eyes on Barnabas before they looked at one another. The silence in the room was deafening, so deep that if the proverbial pin had dropped, it would have sounded like a cannon shot.

"Are you saying that you think someone else is involved?" Branigan rose to walk towards Barnabas.

"I am It makes sick sense, you know?" Barnabas dropped into a nearby chair, unsure if he was even on the right track. "I mean, I share the name with the Foundation. Dad did name it in part after me and in part after the Barnabas in the Bible."

Breck nodded. "We've thought that over the months when we have all been through this stuff. We never did find out who it was for some of what we went through." He began to pace. "We never did figure out who was driving that ATV that ran Neasa and me down."

"No, we didn't." Barnabas rose, heading for a clear whiteboard. "Okay, let's think about this. What would be a motive?"

"Money. Bribe you to pay out money to stop it." Benen spoke first.

"Revenge?" This from Brendon.

"I agree. Who wanted something from the Foundation and never got it?" Baird spoke up.

"Or wanted on the board and was turned down?" Branigan was thinking aloud.

"Or wanted to go out on a mission through the Foundation and was turned down?" Burnie spoke as he rose, heading for Barnabas.

"Someone who felt that they should run one of the charities we deal with?" Bradon looked up from where he was writing on a pad. "If we make a list of the charities and go from there?"

"Talk to Darcie. See if she can profile something for us." Buckley rubbed at his head. "I can do that if you like."

"If you would." Barnabas began to pace before he left the room, heading to find his father. Bruce was in the lobby, speaking with Abe.

"Barnabas?" Abe looked at him before he exchanged a look with Murphy.

"Dad? I had a thought and the fellows are working on it. What if it wasn't Aubrey?" Barnabas drew a deep breath, a bleak look around his eyes. "What if she was taken, to get to me, to get to the Foundation through me? Someone who knows me well enough to know that she was a good friend in college?"

Bruce studied his son. "I had that thought, son. I was just asking Abe about that. Emma will start working on that premise, he tells me. And that Darcie is sending over a profile. She had the same thought."

"Buckley was approaching her about that." Barnabas rubbed at his face. "Maybe I should step back from the Foundation, step back from what I do."

Abe shook his head. "That is likely what they want. If you do that, they win, whoever they are. Let us work through this first. Is Aubrey up to talking to us?"

Barnabas shrugged. "I can see. She was still sleeping when I left this morning." He turned, not even thinking to excuse himself, heading for his apartment.

Hagen looked around as he entered, pointing to the living room, a grin on her face.

"In there. She's been pretty good all morning. The alternating ice packs and heat have been helping. Although right now, she's held captive."

"Captive?" Barnabas grinned as he peeked into the living room.

Aubrey was seated on the couch, her feet and legs up on an ottoman, a blanket covering them. Heath and Hannah stood one on either side of her, competing for her attention. Barnabas grinned as Heath covered Aubrey's face with kisses and then Hannah had to copy her brother. Aubrey's face was alight with laughter before she asked the little ones if she could read.

Heath plopped down beside her, pointing to the book, Hannah standing with an arm around her neck, leaning against her.

"Aube. Read,"

"I will, but you need to listen. Okay?" Aubrey looked up, a huge smile on her face as Barnabas leaned over them to kiss her, one hand on the back of the couch to balance himself.

He began to laugh as Heath pushed at him. "Mine. Aube mine."

"No, she's mine, but I'll share." Barnabas simply picked up the little fellow and sat tight to Aubrey, settling Heath on his knee. "Here. Aubrey will read to us for a bit. Then I think your Mommy is looking for you for your lunch."

"No lunch. Aube read." Heath's bottom lip came out in mutiny.

Aubrey touched it gently. "No lip, Heath, or I don't read. We talked about that."

Hagen finally rescued Aubrey from her twins, laughing at the protest they put up before she headed home. Aubrey's head went down against Barnabas as his arm swept around her.

"Tired?" He watched her face closely.

"I am, but a good tired. Those twins are just so special."

"They are." Barnabas began to laugh. "Heath has certainly claimed you."

"He has. Hagen had a horrible time getting him away from me." She laughed as she remembered the struggles that morning before she sobered. "I just don't want them hurt."

"We'll take care, sweetheart." Barnabas just sat, content for the moment, before he spoke. "We had a thought this morning, sweetheart, that I need to speak with you about. Abe would like to as well,"

Aubrey twisted her head to look at him. "About who is it? I've been thinking about that. There's a list there on the end table of Jeremy and Jason's known contacts. The names of his security guards. It's been so strange what has happened. I can't see that Jeremy profited any by holding me prisoner. And I know that Jason was never around that much. I think that I said Jeremy made sure of that."

"That's what we're thinking. We are now wondering if someone knew how much you meant to me back then, had Jeremy hold you captive, to come after me and through me, the Foundation." He watched her face as she thought through what he had said.

"I have often wondered that very thing, love. I had so much time to think. Is that what you think?"

"It seems to be the consensus. I would hate that this happened to you because of me."

"God knows, love. He knows."

Chapter 30

That evening, Barnabas turned from his home office, a deep sigh drawn from him. They were no further ahead, he decided, and he did not like that one little bit. Lord? This is so hard. Now I understand what the others went through. It doesn't make it any easier. He stood for a moment, deep in thought and prayer before he looked up as Aubrey reached to hug him.

"Love?" She tilted her head to look up at him, deep shadows under her eyes and pain in them.

"You need to be sitting down, sweetheart. You're in pain." He turned her towards the bedroom, intent on tucking her in, but she resisted.

"No, I don't want that. We need to talk, Barnabas. But more than that, we need to pray. I fear for you."

"I know, sweetheart." He tucked her up on the couch. "I'll be right back." He was as good as his word, returning with her tea and his coffee and then sitting beside her, snuggling her tight.

"Have you talked with the fellows?"

"Not since late this afternoon. I don't want to hover over them. They understand, but they don't need that." He sighed again. "I just wish this was over, but it's not. Not by a long shot."

"Me too. Was that list any help?"

"Brendon took it and then copied it for everyone. They will all take a look at it, do what they do best in their research, and then compile a report. They all have different ways of looking at things."

"I know. I gave a copy to Muir when she stopped by this afternoon. She said the ladies were in competition with the men and they had a secret weapon."

Barnabas grinned. "They are and they do? Did she say who?"

"No, she didn't." Aubrey's voice softened as she thought about their conversation before her mind turned to the twins. "Those twins are special, aren't they?"

"They are. Hagen didn't want twins, she said, not sure that she would be able to manage. She has done well. Her sisters help a lot. Brandon is so proud of them. He can't wait to get home at night now, just to be with his family."

"And there are other little ones. I need to get to know them, but I am so hesitant to be around them."

"They understand. The ladies will not deny you an opportunity to see them or the little ones. I know that for a fact. We just need to be careful, that's all."

"Do you think there is someone behind Jeremy? I could never understand why. He never really gave an answer whenever I spoke with him."

"I am sure we are. Who it is? That's what we're working on." Barnabas grew quiet, content he thought for the first time in years.

———

"Your Mom and Dad were around earlier this afternoon. Your Mom is spoiling me."

"She will. They always wanted a daughter but couldn't have any more children. Mom is so happy right now. She will spoil you, I know. You deserve to be."

"No. No, I don't. But I understand why she wants to." Aubrey shifted how she was sitting, to ease the pain in her back. "Where do we go from here, love? How do we find this person or persons?"

"We keep digging. Dallas is digging as well. The new detective, Davy, has been assigned to help him." Barnabas frowned. "He looks familiar."

"Didn't someone say a homeless man named Davy helped Breck? Could it have been him?"

"It may well have been." Barnabas yawned, his fatigue catching up with him. "How be we spend some time in prayer and reading our favourite verses? We haven't been able to for a few days."

Chapter 31

Baird was on a hunt two days later. He had come across some information that he needed to talk to Barnabas about and just could not find him. He paused, a hand rubbing at his neck before he headed for the parking lot and then nodded. Barnabas isn't in the building.

Turning back, Baird headed for Barnabas' apartment, hoping to find Aubrey. He watched as the door opened carefully and Aubrey peeked around it.

"Baird? You're here?"

"I am. I was trying to find Barnabas."

"He's in town. He said it would this evening when he got home. Can I help?"

Baird stared at her. "You know, you might be able to. Are you feeling up to coming to the conference room for a bit?"

"I can. Just let me grab my keys." Aubrey was back in short order, pulling on a cardigan. She stared down at her feet. "I can't change my slippers, though."

"That doesn't matter." Baird held out an arm for Aubrey to take, to give her balance if she needed it.

Aubrey stared around the room, amazed at how much activity was going on. "Those boards. They have a lot more information than when I last saw them."

"There is." Bradon had approached. "How are you today, Aubrey?"

She shrugged her attention not on him but on the boards. She moved that way, not seeing the looks the men exchanged. Bradon followed her, watching her closely.

Aubrey stopped, her finger on a name. "Who is this?"

"That is Jeremy's ex-wife. Jason's mother. Did you ever meet her?"

"No, but I have heard that name. I just can't remember where." Aubrey was frustrated at that.

"It will come to you." Bradon studied her face. "You've thought of something."

"I have. I just don't know how to express it." Aubrey found a chair to sit in, her back starting to ache. "How do I do that?"

"Just start talking. I can take notes or we can record your thoughts." Bradon reached for the laptop near her, bringing up a word processing program and pointing to the little microphone icon. "We can use this or you can use your phone."

"This works." Aubrey bit at her lip, not sure how to proceed. "Okay. So, I just start talking?"

Bradon grinned at her. "You do. Would you like me to find Heath and Hannah and you can pretend to be reading them a story?"

Aubrey stared at him before her eyes narrowed. "Funny man, aren't you? Hagen must have talked."

"Actually it was your husband who did. He was laughing as he told us about the other day."

"Those twins are quite the pair. Brandon and Hagen will have their hands full in the future." Aubrey smirked at Brandon as he grinned at her.

"That we will, Aubrey. But Heath is insistent that he needs his Aube and so does Hannah."

"I love those two little ones. Now, to go back to what I was thinking. I guess I have to go back to when Mom was still alive."

"Go back to where you need to." Burnie had moved closer, a pen and paper ready to take notes. "I'll listen and jot down what I think is important or what we would need to question further."

Aubrey finally nodded, her mind slipping back in time, back to when she was about sixteen. She knew Jeremy had been around, trying to get her mother to sign paperwork. Her mother had told him to leave and not return, that she would not sign any paperwork he presented. Aubrey had asked her mother about him and had been told to avoid him.

Her mind drifted forward, to when she was eighteen and her mother slipped away from her overnight. Aubrey had been in shock, not realizing that Jeremy had stepped in, taking over. She had turned to her friends and her own lawyer, leaning on them.

Aubrey came back to the present, her eyes on the men gathered around. "He was never my guardian. I was eighteen when Mom died. I had my own lawyer and he would have told me. He didn't."

"Let me know your lawyer's name and I'll contact him." Branigan reached for the paper she had written on. "I'll do that later. For now, continue, Aubrey."

Chapter 32

Aubrey began to speak, her voice low at times, as her mind traced back to her university days. Breck nodded at some of her comments, a frown in place at other times.

Knowing that her mother would have wanted her to complete her education, Aubrey had struggled with finances, working hard and long over the summers, finding grants when she could, not wanting to go into debt if she could avoid that. She had known that Jeremy had been hovering around at the edge of her life and she learned quickly how to watch for him and to not let him near her if she could at all help it.

She had treasured her growing friendship with Barnabas, falling fast and deeply in love with him, not expecting that he would ever return her love. When, during their last few months of school, he had approached her, asking if she would consider moving to his town, that he wanted to explore their friendship and see if she felt the same as he did, she had agreed. What she hadn't known was that Jason had been nearby and had gone to his father.

Jeremy had begun to plan at that point, to plan how to trap her. She hadn't suspected anything when she had been asked if she wanted to work with some young children at a home. Seeing as it was her line of work, she had agreed, planning on only staying for the requested two months and then moving to Barnabas' town.

Once there, she had been imprisoned by Jeremy. No amount of pleading or escaping had worked. If she got out, he found her and dragged her back. Doors were locked from the outside. Windows were sealed shut. She was allowed her phone and internet access but under direct threat to those that she would communicate with. Her calls and emails from Barnabas had been the highlight of her weeks until Jeremy had decided that he would end those. She had been asleep the night the lock was installed on her bedroom door.

Aubrey had pleaded and sobbed with him to let her out, but he didn't respond. Two years had gone by, two years of despair alternating with hope. She had tried to think of everyone who might be involved, writing them down. She had researched the Foundation in the past, remembering the name of a lawyer involved who Barnabas had mentioned on occasion. That information she had mailed to him, somehow getting it out. She still wasn't sure how that had happened. The envelope had been on her dresser one day and then gone the next.

Having kept a copy secreted, Aubrey had frequently pulled it out and added to it as she could. She came back to the present, finding the men watching her closely.

"That list, Aubrey. Do you still have it?"

"I do. But I don't need a written list." She began to name names, listing what she knew about them.

Breck frowned at a couple of the names. "Does Dallas have these?"

Aubrey shrugged. "John has most of them. I don't know if he handed them over. I didn't ask him that."

"I know about four of them. They are from here. Now, that makes sense. If someone is trying to get to the Foundation, they would need someone from this area, now wouldn't they?"

"Tell us which ones, Breck, and we'll concentrate on those. Male or female?" Bradon looked up from his notes.

"Both." Breck named them, seeing the men exchange glances. "We all know them, I think. Barnabas has had a run-in with the men over the years regarding the Foundation." He paused, lost in thought for a moment. "I think that he was right. That Jeremy was working for someone to get to Aubrey and through Aubrey to Barnabas and then the Foundation."

"It makes sick sense." Baird looked around at the other men. "I have had my own difficulties with one of the men. About a couple of years after I moved here. He wanted me to provide documents for him, documents that I had no access to. I told him no, walked away, and never thought much about it. I did talk to Bruce at the time."

"That's strange. I think he has approached all of us, am I correct?" Buckley looked around, seeing the nods. "The last time was what, about two years ago?"

"That would be it." Brady looked up as Aubrey gave a sound. "About the time that you were locked up tight?"

"About that. Oh, no! He was using me." There was devastation on Aubrey's face. "I didn't know."

"No, you wouldn't." Buckley sat beside her. "Aubrey, what else can you tell us?"

She shrugged. "Not much more." She frowned. "I don't know how Jeremy made it as a lawyer. I don't remember that he had an office. He was around the house a lot the first few years, barely on the phone with clients. He has a loud voice and I could hear him clearly."

"Okay. We can look into that. I can talk with John if I have your permission." Breck studied her. "In fact, I think it's a good idea if we did that."

"Sure. Whatever it takes." Aubrey rose, excusing herself, her back beginning to be painful.

Brady followed her as she walked back to the apartment, keeping an eye on her gait. Please heal her, Lord. And help us to bring whoever it is to justice.

———

Chapter 33

Aubrey had wandered the apartment that evening, worried that Barnabas had not returned. She squinted at the clock on the mantle. It was after seven and no word from him. She reached for her phone, scrolling through her messages. Not a one from him since mid-afternoon.

She sighed, stretching out on the couch, a hot water bottle against her back, a cold pack on the coffee table. She eyes the glass of ginger ale that she had sat there and shaken her head. No, she didn't want it. Aubrey had found some crackers early, hoping they would suffice until Barnabas was home. Elizabeth had been around earlier, her concern for Aubrey having been uppermost in her mind.

Awakening, Aubrey sat up abruptly, not sure what had roused her. She was on her feet, heading for the door, hearing the knocking that seemed to be getting louder and louder. She peeked through the peephole and then unlocked the door, swinging it open for Breck and Neasa to enter.

"Breck? Neasa?" She stared between the two, seeing the grim look on Breck's face and the compassion on Neasa's. Fear drove a sharp pain into her heart. "No, he's not. Please, God. No! Not that!"

Breck's hand came out to steady her. "He's in the hospital, Aubrey. I don't have a lot of details, other than we need to bring you in. Dress warmly. It's starting to sleet and the wind is cold."

Aubrey stared at him before Neasa touched her arm.

"Aubrey? Where are your boots? Your coat?"

Aubrey turned, moving as quickly as she was able to, heading for the bedroom, struggling into her coat and picking up the backpack she preferred to a purse. She stared down at her feet, reaching to pull off the pair of Barnabas' heavy wool socks that she had put on earlier, heading back for the closet in the hall, to pull on her boots.

Breck's hand was under her arm, Neasa's arm linked with her as they walked as rapidly as they could for Breck's truck.

Aubrey stared out of the side window as she listened to Breck and Neasa's conversation about the roads. Breck was glad that he had an all-wheel-drive on his truck, but the slick roads still meant he needed to be cautious.

Neasa turned to watch Aubrey, concern on her face.

"Aubrey?"

Aubrey turned her gaze to Neasa. "Neasa, what do you know?"

"Not a lot, Aubrey. I was called by a patrol officer. They couldn't raise you on your phone. I was just told that he was found in a parking lot and had been hurt. That they needed you to come as quickly as you could." Breck's eyes watched her for a moment in the rearview mirror.

"He was outside? In this?" Aubrey was horrified. "Who? How?"

"That we don't know, Aubrey. They didn't say much." Breck pulled to a stop near the entrance to the Emergency Department. "Stay put, Aubrey. Let me come around and help you. You won't do Barnabas any good if you fall in your rush to get to him." Breck was as good as his word, around the truck, helping Neasa out and then Aubrey and then walking them to the door, watching carefully as they entered before he moved quickly to park his truck.

Hearing his name called, Breck paused, his shoulder hunching up towards his face as he turned. Bruce and Elizabeth were coming towards him.

"Breck? I just got the call. We were in town at a dinner. How is he?" Bruce reached for Breck's arm. "Aubrey?"

"I just got her in. Neasa's with her. I haven't been told much, other than he was found outside in a parking lot and unresponsive."

"No!" Elizabeth's hands covered her mouth. "No, please, Lord!"

The three found Neasa and Aubrey seated in the waiting room. Aubrey was on the edge of her seat, her knee bouncing with her frustration and anxiety. Elizabeth dropped to the seat beside her, an arm around her.

"Aubrey? Any word?"

Aubrey shook her head, a hand wiping at the tears on her face. "Not yet. They said that they'd come to get me. He is still being assessed." Her tortured eyes raised to Bruce who had crouched down in front of her. "Why?"

"I understand they are working on that, Aubrey. They will want to speak with Barnabas when he awakens. Can I get you anything?"

"No, thank you. Just find who it is." She looked up at Breck. "Breck?"

"We're working on those names, Aubrey. I spoke with both John and Dallas. John said that you wanted to sign something that day he spoke with you that would let him speak with us."

"I did. Barnabas and I had talked about it." She was on her feet, moving towards the physician as he beckoned for her to follow him, her limp pronounced.

Chapter 34

Aubrey moved with the physician towards the room where they had placed Barnabas, stopping at his hand on her arm.

"Aubrey? May I call you that?" At her nod, he continued. "Now, I am not sure what all you have been told. Barnabas was found outside, just as the rain was turning to sleet. He's suffering from hypothermia, among other things."

"What else, doctor?" Aubrey's eyes did not move from the closed door.

"He was beaten, by the looks of it. He has numerous nicks and cuts on his face and hand, from the window that was broken."

"Broken window?" Aubrey's eyes shot to him. "What are you talking about?"

"The patrol officer who came in with him said that the driver's window was shattered. We don't know why or by whom." He paused, drawing in a deep breath. "At the moment, we are working to warm Barnabas back up. I won't go into all the details, not until later. As a start, he has been to imaging. He has deep bruising along the left side of his body. No rib fracture that we can see. But he is in critical condition, Aubrey."

Aubrey paled even more. "Critical? Oh, no!" She looked up at the physician, devastation on her face. "Can I please go to him?"

"You can but before you do I need to let you know what you will find. He is on oxygen, warmed to help heat his interior core. Heated intravenous. He is wrapped in warming blankets. Barnabas has not awakened as yet nor responded to us." The physician watched with compassion as Aubrey wiped at her face. "You can stay for a while, Aubrey, but we will need you to leave from time to time. Have you family here?"

"Just his parents. I'm an orphan. And good friends. Breck brought me in."

"Breck and Neasa? Good. Anything else that I can get you right now?"

"Just whoever it was that did this." Aubrey walked away from towards the stretcher that held Barnabas, a hand covering her mouth as she stared down at him. Please, Lord? Heal him. I just don't understand why.

She laid her hand against his cheek, feeling the chill on it. Bending, Aubrey kissed him, her tears splashing against his face. She stood even as the nurses and therapists worked around her, trying to warm Barnabas. It was a slow process, they told her. As soon as he was stable enough, they would move him to a floor.

"ICU?" Aubrey's voice was barely a whisper.

"It might be. We'll see how he comes around." The charge nurse smiled at Aubrey, her eyes compassionate. "Right now, though, we need you to step back into the waiting room. We'll come to get you in a bit."

Aubrey bent to kiss Barnabas on the cheek once more, her hand lingering on his jaw, before she turned, walking away, her steps slow and halting as she made her way back to the waiting room. She knew that she would need to give an answer to the unspoken questions but she hesitated just outside the doors, her eyes on the floor. Tears trickled down her face.

Bruce was waiting for her and simply reached to hug her, holding her as she wept before he turned her back to where Elizabeth sat. He simply shook his head at his wife as Aubrey sat beside her.

"Aubrey?" Elizabeth shared a look with Neasa and Breck when the younger woman didn't answer. "Did you see Barnabas?"

Aubrey nodded. "I did. He's not waking up." She swiped at her face, mad at herself that she was weeping but unable to stop herself. "They're trying to warm him up from inside the doctor said." She looked around at them. "Why? Why Barnabas? Who hates him that much?"

Bruce wrapped her in his arms as he would have his own daughter and became to pray for her. When he was done, he watched her face before he rose and motioned to Breck.

"Bruce?" Breck was curious as to what Bruce was thinking.

"Have we considered that? What Aubrey said?"

"That someone hates Barnabas that much? The fellows and I have discussed that. Buckley and Branigan have made it their concentrated duty to look into that." Breck hesitated, not sure how to continue. "He would send us out, teams of six, when he needed to, to bring people or information back that was needed. He hasn't done that since the fellows went in and brought Baird and Berneen out."

"I wonder if it's something to do with that. Do you know the circumstances on those?"

Breck shook his head. "He would tell us what we needed to know. He often never said who had requested that."

"No, he wouldn't. He would keep it quiet so as not to break a confidence." Bruce paced as Breck divided his attention between Bruce and the three ladies. "I'll have to see what I can find out. He keeps things confidential and I will not break that trust."

Breck watched as Aubrey as she spoke with a nurse before she turned, distress in her demeanour.

"Bruce. I think something has happened." Breck nodded towards Aubrey. "Aubrey was just speaking with a nurse."

"She was?" Bruce had spun and was across the room, his arm around his daughter-in-law. "Aubrey?"

"They're transferring him to the ICU, they said. He still hasn't awakened. She said it was not unusual, but I hate this. I really do." Aubrey leaned against Bruce as she wept, afraid that Barnabas would never wake up and would indeed slip away from her forever.

Chapter 35

Waking up during the night, Bruce looked around at the ICU waiting room. Elizabeth sat beside him, her head on his shoulder, her hand in his. Breck was slumped on a couch, his arm around Neasa as she curled up beside him, a sheet that he had found wrapped around her. Both were sound asleep. Bruce's eyes turned to Aubrey and he gave a sad smile. Aubrey was curled up on another couch, her backpack as a pillow. Elizabeth had found a blanket to cover her with before she had stood, hand on Aubrey's head, and prayed for the younger woman. Bruce sighed, his heart raising in petition to their God, asking that Barnabas would awaken and if he didn't that they would have peace. He knew the dangers of hypothermia even at this stage.

Aubrey roused, sitting up and pushing her hair away from her face before she was on her feet heading towards the doors to the unit. She had sought and been granted permission to enter when she could. The nurses had looked at her and then one another. They only knew too well the dangers that faced the young couple.

Standing beside Barnabas, Aubrey stared at the equipment surrounding him, frowning. She wasn't quite sure but she felt that he had improved. Her eyes dropped to his beloved face before she stooped to kiss him.

"Please, Lord? I need my best friend, my husband, my soul mate. Please, Lord? Don't let him die." She stood with a hand on his cheek, before she began to speak again. "Barnabas, I love you so much, more and more each moment. We tell each other that in words and actions. I can't handle it if you do leave me. Please, love? Wake up for me?"

She finally turned away, not seeing the flickering of Barnabas' eyelids as he tried to rouse before he slipped back into the darkness. Bruce was standing waiting for her, an arm out to hug her as he turned her back to the waiting room.

"Aubrey?" His voice was low as he spoke.

"About the same, Bruce." She drew a deep shaking breath. "I'm so afraid."

"I know, Aubrey. I know. We are too. But he is still here. God had not chosen to take him home yet."

"No, but He could at any time." Aubrey dropped back to the couch before looking up at the older man. "How do we do this? Have we heard anything?"

"Not yet. Will Peters was around earlier. He's the police chief whom I am not sure that you have met yet."

"No, I don't think I have. I have heard the fellows talk about him. Did he know anything?"

"He didn't say much other than they had the truck towed to their garage and the techs and mechanic would be going over it in the morning." Bruce sat beside her, a hand reaching for hers as he began to pray for her.

Breck had roused as they spoke before he shook his head. Lord, he thought, this is getting old. We need our friend. Please, Lord? He has taught us so much on how to live for You and for each other. Please, dear Lord? Barnabas and I have been friends for so long there would be a gap in my life if he wasn't in it. I mean, our friendship has changed with us each married but we still need one another. He's my brother that I never had.

Will Peters stood for a moment, eying the five in the waiting room before he approached Aubrey. Bruce had looked up at the footsteps and was on his feet, his face turning grim.

"Will, you're here?"

"I am, Bruce. As a friend, not in my normal capacity. This is Aubrey?" He sat beside her, a hand out to shake hers. He introduced himself and then watched her, seeing the fragility that she was trying hard to hide. It's not just this, is it, Lord? It's more and more what's going on. And that we still have not figured out totally.

"Hi." Aubrey eyes him carefully. "You shouldn't be here."

"But I should. Bruce and I have been friends for years. I watched Barnabas grow up. He's an important part of my life. I can't be anywhere else. But what can we do for you, Aubrey?"

She shrugged, turning her eyes to the hands that she had clasped together in her lap, her diamond engagement ring catching her attention. "Find who did this. Find who it is that is behind it all. I think." Her voice died away. "I think that whoever it is has been using me. They knew that we were important to one another. Likely because he was the only one I was getting mail or phone calls from. Jeremy was likely monitoring that without me being aware of it. They are after him. Why?"

"That's what we are all working on, Aubrey. I think Dallas will likely be around tomorrow or later today to talk with you. He said he had something that he needed to verify. And no, I don't know what it is. I keep hands off from their work unless I need to step in. He has the new detective, Davy, working with him."

"I see." Aubrey grew quiet before her eyes closed and she slept. Will stood, shifting her so that she once more laid on the couch and reached to cover her.

"Will? What didn't you say?" Bruce knew his friend well.

"Nothing that is definite, Bruce. Just a question that I had." Will sat down in a chair near where Elizabeth was still sleeping, watching as Bruce sat beside his wife. "I think Aubrey hit the nail on the head with her comment."

"Someone using her to get to Barnabas?"

"That. It has never made sense that she was kept captive unless she was a pawn in a huge horrible game of chess that just doesn't end. There has been no checkmate yet."

"No, there has not been and that is worrisome. Elizabeth is not sleeping at night like she needs to."

"None of us are. I talked with Barnabas a few days ago. He is worried about Aubrey, and I think that concern is legitimate. How we go forward with this has many avenues. Dallas and Davy are working on some. Davy has a lot of resources that he can turn to."

"Davy? As in the Davy that found Breck?" Bruce nodded when Will didn't comment, just watched him. "I see. Then we need to pray, my friend. My son is in critical condition because someone chose to attack him and leave him to die. I want that person. I want to stand in front of whoever it is and ask why, what did he ever do to them?"

Chapter 36

Standing beside Barnabas' bed two nights later, Aubrey watched him closely. They had been able to move him to a regular room, he had improved enough that they had been able to do that. He still had not roused and that scared Aubrey. She looked around, then lowered the bedrail and crawled up beside him, an arm under his shoulders as much as she could, her other hand on his cheek even as she kissed him, feeling the growth of beard under her lips, and then laid her head on his shoulders. She slept, not seeing the woman who stopped in the doorway or the look of rage on her face. Their enemy had tracked them down.

The night nurse paused for a moment before she shook her head. I would likely do the same thing, she thought, and turned and headed to find a heated sheet that she tucked tight around Aubrey. She continued with her duties and then left, stopping to frown at the woman standing down the hall. It was after visiting hours, she thought, and walked towards her. The woman shot an angry look at her and then almost ran for the stairs, heading out and away from the hospital, pausing beside a younger man who was waiting near the entrance to the parking lot. He nodded as she spoke to him before he headed for the hospital, his employee card swiped in the lock, allowing him entrance.

His eyelids flickering, Barnabas gradually returned to his senses. His eyes cracked open as he peeked around. A hospital room? What did I go and do, he wondered? What happened to me? I hurt all over and it is difficult to breathe. He shifted his position, a weight on his shoulder holding him still for a moment. He frowned before his face softened and the hand with the IV in it lifted to brush the deep red curls from Aubrey's face. His hand then rested on her arm as his face turned towards her as much as it could and he slept, this time a natural sleep.

The young man stood in the doorway, looking towards the nurses' station before he entered, anger on his face. He stood over Barnabas and then turned and walked away, knowing that he could do nothing at that point. The woman would have to wait, that's what he decided.

Aubrey roused as the nurses began their morning rounds, rubbing at her nose before she raised her head, finding herself facing Barnabas. She frowned for a moment before her face lit up. His eyes were open and he was smiling at her, as much as she could see through the oxygen mask covering his lower face.

"Love, you're awake! Oh, praise God1"

Barnabas' hand traced her cheek before he reached to pull down the mask, kissing her.

"Barnabas, put that back on." Aubrey's face was rosy even as she reached to replace the mask.

"Are you okay?" His hand reached to pull the mask back down.

"I am. You're not. Now, behave." She looked up as she heard steps and found the physician standing there. "Dr. White? He's awake!"

"So I see. How be you pop down off the bed and head out to the waiting room? Just long enough for us to check him over. You can come back, I promise." He watched with compassion the struggle that Aubrey went through before she nodded, reached to kiss Barnabas, and then was off the bed, heading for the waiting room.

Bruce looked up as she almost danced towards him and was on his feet, hope on his face.

"Aubrey?"

"He's awake, Bruce. He's awake. Oh, Dad! God is good. Barnabas is awake!" She threw herself into his arms, feeling his tight hug and then hearing his prayer of thankfulness.

Bruce blinked back tears of happiness before he thought through what Aubrey had said. He paused and then smiled. She had called him "Dad". They had asked her to do that and she had refused until now.

"What does the doctor say?"

"He kicked me out so that he could examine him." Aubrey spun, whirling around the room in her happiness. "I can go back in when he's done. You're coming with me." She paused in front of him. "Mom. You need to call Mom and let her know. Please?"

Bruce simply hugged her again and reached for his phone, to do just that, handing her his phone.

When Elizabeth answered, all she heard was silence for a moment and her heart fell until she heard the happy voice wafting across the airwaves.

"Mom? He's awake. Barnabas is awake and talking. God heard!" Aubrey's voice could hardly contain all the happiness she felt.

"He is? Oh, praise the Lord. Aubrey. Is Bruce with you?"

"Dad is. Thank you, Mom. Can you come?"

"I can and will. Let me talk to Bruce for a moment?"

Bruce took his phone back and moved away, turning to watch Aubrey as she stood, arms wrapped around herself and praying, he knew.

"Bruce?"

"Yes, Elizabeth. He is awake and talking she says."

"Oh, thank God. But she called me "Mom"?" Elizabeth's voice had uncertainty and yet joy.

"She did. I'm Dad to her now. She didn't realize that what was she had called us, I don't think."

"It doesn't matter. It shows that she is healing and beginning to live again. I'm on my way."

"Wait, hon. Breck sent a text that he was heading in about this time. He offered to stop by and bring you in."

"He did? Oh, okay." Elizabeth peeked through the window of the door. "He's here now. See you in a bit." Elizabeth just opened the door and hugged Breck.

Breck stood for a moment before he hugged her back, not sure what was happening.

"Elizabeth?"

Elizabeth stood back, wiping at her eyes, causing Breck's heart to fall.

"Aubrey called us Mom and Dad." She laughed, a happy laugh filled with tears. "She also told me that Barnabas is awake and has spoken."

"Oh, praise the Lord! Well? What are we waiting for?" He grinned at her, a grin he used to give when he was a teen and wanting her to go with him somewhere. "Are you up for a fast trip through town?"

"I am and this time, I won't complain if you speed. Neasa is with you?"

"She is." Breck helped Elizabeth down the sidewalk to the truck and then into the back of the cab. "Neasa, Barnabas has woken up."

Chapter 37

Four days later, Barnabas sank into his chair in his home office, staring at the pile of folders and mail awaiting him. He sighed. He didn't feel up to it but knew he needed to make a start. Aubrey watched him before she set his mug of coffee beside him, standing with an arm around his shoulders.

"You need help with this. What can I do?"

Barnabas looked up, a grateful look on his face. "Dad and Amy have done what they could with Breck's help. But these?" He lifted a corner of the pile of file folders and then let it drop. "These are what I need to go through."

"And you don't feel like it. Let me help. Where do we start?"

Two hours later, Barnabas sat back, exhausted but content. With Aubrey's help, he had sorted through what he needed to accomplish, done just that, and then had sat and watched as she sat, her hair disheveled from running her hands through it as she answered the last of the letters for him.

"Thanks, sweetheart. I didn't think that we would get through all this."

Aubrey looked up, a smile on her face. "We did. I just need you to sign these and I can take them out for mailing."

He watched as she walked away before he pulled up his email, his face paling as he read the email that he had received. This is vicious, he thought. Whoever it is doesn't threaten Aubrey. They threaten me, and then her if she gets in the way. I don't get why. He sighed to himself as he forwarded the email on to Dallas.

Dallas had been around two days before, his eyes watchful as he studied the waiting room, taking in the visitors sitting there, in particular, one couple who seemed out of place and uncomfortable. He had taken a photo of them and sent it on to Davy, asking that he try and confirm identities. He was surprised at how quickly Davy had responded, giving their names and then asking why? When informed, Davy had simply stated that he was on his way, if that was okay with his boss. Dallas had grinned. Even though Davy was slightly older than himself, they were comfortable working as a team.

Barnabas had looked up as Dallas had entered his room, a nod greeting him before his eyes dropped to Aubrey, who was curled up against him once more, sound asleep. He had smiled, a somewhat sad smile as he watched her.

"Dallas? How many times have you been around?"

"Enough that the nurses just look past me. How are you?" Dallas pulled up a chair near the table, his laptop coming out as did his portable printer.

"Getting there. Not something that I would recommend for anyone, that's for sure." Barnabas' head went back. He still hurt all over, partly from the beating that he had undergone. "Where do I start, Dallas?"

"From early that day, I would think." Dallas watched him closely. "Your heart is hurting, my friend."

"It is. I know that Aubrey is being threatened. I want whoever it is to answer for that. Only I don't see that will happen."

"We're doing our best. Your Dad picked up your truck. Will authorized it. He's taken it in to have the window replaced." Dallas paused as Barnabas' head shot up and he stared at him.

"The window?"

"It was shattered. Don't you remember? Your face, at least the left side, took a beating from the shattered glass.

Barnabas' eyes closed. "I do remember that now that you have mentioned it." He looked down for a moment, his hand rubbing at his chest. "I need to give you my statement and I'm not sure I should with Aubrey here."

"She's asleep?"

"She is and she will need to find out what happened. I'm just not sure if I'm ready to tell her. Not like this."

"She's a lot stronger than any of us give her credit for. You know that, Barnabas. She told me yesterday that she was mad at God for letting this happen. That she needed you to continue to teach her how to live.”

"She said that? I can’t have her mad at God. Not at all. And I guess if hearing what happens fixes that, I have to let her hear.”

Chapter 38

Barnabas thought back to that morning. He had taken reluctant leave from Aubrey, seeing the lost look in her eyes that she quickly shuttered. Knowing that he would be away all day, he had hugged and kissed her, promising to text or call as he could. Barnabas had walked away, heading first to do some shopping, his list of Christmas presents for Aubrey quickly finished. He had stared at the florist and decided to stop in on his way home, hoping that it would still be open.

His meetings finished, he had headed for the florist shop, finding it still open and quickly purchasing the daisies and carnations that he knew she liked from their university days. He had headed home, stopping at an out-of-the-way store to make an impulse purchase. The box tucked into a pocket, he had headed for his truck, his coat collar turned up against the cold rain that lashed at him.

Barnabas had pulled out of his parking spot, the last to leave, he thought, delayed by a phone call. Even the store that he had just exited was dark, everyone heading home. He had slammed on his brakes as someone appeared in front of him and then he took a look in the rearview mirror. He sighed. Someone just had to appear there, now didn't they?

He had flinched as a hand banged at his window before an iron bar kept hitting at it, finally shattering it. His arm had gone up in reflex, to protect him as much as he could from the pieces of glass. A hand had reached in, unlocking his door. A voice had ordered him to put the truck in park. When he refused, the man reached angrily across him to do just that.

Pulled roughly from the vehicle, he had stood watching the men, trying his best to get as much of a description of them as he could, to no avail. Woollen hats pulled down as much as possible and scarves wrapped around the lower faces prevented that, that and the stinging rain that lashed at him. He had sensed movement to his left side and tried to move away, the iron bar meeting his ribs and driving him to his knees where a second blow to the same area dropped him to the ground. He lay, an arm wrapped around himself, drawing in ragged breathes, unable to understand the words driven at him. He had felt the kicks driven into his legs before he was on his own, his vision fading as he passed out.

Not knowing if he was still alone or not, Barnabas had roused, pain lashing through him still. He had pushed himself up with one arm, bracing himself to stay sitting up. His other arm was wrapped around his chest to try and ease the pain. He had drawn up his legs, his feet slipping on the wet pavement as he tried to rise, unable to get traction to do so. Barnabas had raised his head, his eyes closing against the cold rain that was changing over to stinging sleet. Unable to stay upright, his arm had begun shaking until it could no longer support him. He slipped back to the pavement, his head hitting hard before blackness overwhelmed him and he slipped away into that dark well of forgetfulness. He didn't feel the cold driving his body to shiver and then past that as hypothermia set in.

How long he lay there, they were never quite sure. A patrol officer had pulled in, seeing the truck. Running the plates, he was out of it as he was advised that it belonged to Barnabas. A flashlight held high, he had walked around it, stopping as he stared at the open driver's door and the shattered window. He turned, the large light slashed through the darkness, moving across Barnabas' still form and then quickly moving back. The officer was on his radio, calling for help before he was on his knees, hands reaching to assess Barnabas. A quick return to his car had him retrieving the emergency blanket, spreading it over Barnabas to help keep him warm. Keeping him dry was not an option.

His supervisor stood beside him, having heard the call and the name.

"What do you know?"

The officer shook his head. "Not a lot. I saw the truck, came in to check it out, found out how it belonged to, and then found him." He watched closely as the paramedics worked on Barnabas and then moved to help them lift the stretcher into the back of the rig, seeing the grim looks on their faces.

"Do we have any idea how long?" The senior paramedic questioned him even as he reached for the heart monitor.

"No, I don't. Sorry. I found him about ten minutes ago. He's been there for a while I would say."

Rolling the stretcher quickly into the Emergency Department, the paramedics were ready with their report, helping to shift Barnabas to a stretcher in the department before they left. It was a busy night and there were just too many calls, they thought.

Medical staff worked quickly to stabilize Barnabas, the imaging and testing done that was requested, and then the work began to gradually warm him up. They exchanged glances, all of them unsure that he would even make it.

Barnabas finally looked up, shaking his head at Dallas' words as he informed Barnabas of what had transpired. He looked down at Aubrey as she slept. He frowned and then smiled. Faking it, sweetheart. Just so you don't get asked to leave me.

"Do you know who?" Barnabas hoped that the men responsible had been arrested and the burden having over him had been removed.

"No. No, we don't. We have taken the security feed from the stores but it's not much help. The cameras were iced up."

"So, we are no further ahead." Barnabas shook his head. "I want this over, Dallas, and now."

"I know you do, my friend. I wish the same. We're working on some leads, but they are few and far between. Even our contacts on the streets have no idea who or why." Dallas sorted out his papers, had Barnabas sign his statement, and then packed everything away. He hesitated for a moment and then shook his head, moving quickly to the door and then out of the hospital. He stood, his face raised to the sky, questioning why it was not evident who it was.

Aubrey sat up, her eyes on Barnabas as he stared across the room before she just reached to hug him.

"You heard?" Barnabas's voice was low.

"I did. Who is it?"

"That's what I can't figure out. Whoever it is has a vicious streak. They had to know that my life was in danger by leaving me there." He looked up, devastation on his face. "I can't think of anyone, sweetheart."

"When you get home, we'll start listing everyone who has reacted negatively to you. I think Breck and Bradon were working on that."

"I'm sure they are. Do you know when I can leave?"

"In a day or so. They just want to ensure you're healthy enough to."

Chapter 39

Coming back to the present, Barnabas reached for a pad of paper and a pen and began listing names and what he could remember about each one. He vaguely heard Aubrey speaking with someone and looked up before he shrugged and looked back down at his list. He sat back at long last, lifting his eyes to find Branigan and Baird watching him.

"How long have you been here?" Barnabas shook his head. He needed to do better. He could lose himself in his work. That didn't help when someone was after him.

"About fifteen minutes." The two men exchanged glances even as Branigan spoke. "Aubrey said you were involved in something, just what she wasn't sure, and that we could come and just sit and wait for you."

"She said that?" Barnabas shook his head. "I'm sorry. I was listing names and what I could remember. I hadn't done that yet." He handed over his list. "Take a copy of that for everyone."

Branigan reached for it and then headed for the printer to copy enough for all. He was concerned, he had to admit, that Barnabas had ignored them. He would need to speak with Breck, he decided.

Baird took his copy of the list and glanced through it, nodding as he did so. It had to be God, he decided. They were finding all the same names. That didn't happen by chance.

Barnabas watched them and then looked towards the doorway as Aubrey appeared, a tray in her hands. Branigan reached for it, a quiet comment to her before she nodded and looked towards Barnabas.

"Sweetheart?" Barnabas was on his feet, walking towards her even as she backed away. "What is it?"

"I just wanted you to know that I left some sandwiches in the fridge if you fellows get hungry. I'm off to bed."

She walked into his hug, his kiss on her lips before she stepped back, her eyes on him before she turned and walked away. Fear was in her heart. Fear for him. She knew it was only going to get worse and that scared her. She knew what Jeremy was capable of, she had lived that for so many years. But the ones behind him? They were vicious and had little regard for anyone's life. They had proven that with what they had just done.

Barnabas watched her walk away before he turned, hesitating for a moment. He headed for the kitchen, finding the tray of food that she had left, a smile crossing his face for a moment. Baird stood watching him before he reached for the tray.

"Aubrey takes care of you, Barnabas."

"She is learning how to live again, Baird. So much was taken from her that she will never get back. And I am at a loss as to how to help her do just that." Sadness crossed Barnabas' face as he spoke.

———

175

"We know, my friend. We know that. But we see the change in her over the last few days. She has become very protective of you."

"She has?" Barnabas shook his head. "I don't see that."

"That's because you weren't awake." Baird grinned even as he headed back for the office, Branigan clearing a spot on the coffee table for the tray. "We lived it with her when you were unconscious. She was aggressive in ways that we didn't expect. Questioning. Having us research. The ladies spent a lot of time with her, as much as she would allow. Breck talked with your Dad. She tried to look after him and your Mom as well."

"She had that nurturing spirit in school. We all saw that. Jeremy drove it deep inside her. I'm glad it's coming out." Barnabas bit into his sandwich, chewed, swallowed, and then looked at his friends. "Where do we stand on the investigation? I know that you have all pulled back from your work. You don't have to say a word."

"We have." Branigan wiped his mouth on a paper napkin before he continued. "We have eliminated Jeremy has to be responsible for the attack on you. We've talked to people who knew him. Andy flew Brandon and Blair up there. They came back with more information regarding him. That included names from here."

"Names that you aren't willing to share or can share?" Barnabas looked between the two.

"We can. There are four names, two male, two female, that Breck zeroed in on. He says that you have had problems with them. I had issues with one of the men at one point." Baird hesitated.

"The one who wanted the papers from you?" At Baird's nod, Barnabas sat back, his sandwich forgotten in his hand. "I can't see what he wanted those for. They were just researching on a property that went nowhere."

Branigan looked up at that. "Property? Was the board looking at buying it?"

Barnabas shook his head. "No. It was next door to a property that they were looking at purchasing and then decided not to. There had been legal issues of improper lot lines and they didn't feel that they wanted to subject the Foundation to lawsuits over it."

"Okay. So, he wanted it to sue?"

"That's a possibility, I guess. There would not have been anything in it for him. He was the aggressor in it, building over the line and then claiming it as his property. I heard that whoever bought it sued him and he had a huge expense to undo what he had built." Barnabas rubbed at his face. "I don't get why he would be after me, though. I wasn't involved in that. I didn't even have that paperwork."

"We know. Your Dad clarified that. He had been the one involved, he said." Baird paused. "Unless they thought that going after you would get to your father?"

Barnabas paled. "Now that makes sense, doesn't it? Dad's the one who set up the Foundation. He had all this money that he didn't know what to do with and wanted to do something for God. If they could sully his name, it would go against the Foundation, now wouldn't it?"

"It would. Baird, I think that you just found the missing link that we were looking for." Branigan rose, heading for the desk to retrieve a pad of paper and pen before he sat back down. "That list you just gave us? How many of those would have something against your father?"

"The list? Everyone single one. I wasn't thinking that way but it's true." Barnabas bowed his head, his heart praying for his father, knowing that he would need to talk with him and not quite sure how to proceed.

"Let's pray for you and Bruce, Barnabas." Blair didn't wait for a response, simply began to pray.

Chapter 40

Bruce studied his son the next morning as he paced his father's office. His arms on his desk, he rolled a pen under the fingers of one hand, not sure what Barnabas was bothered by.

"Son?"

"Dad? I need to talk to you and I'm not even how to begin." Barnabas dropped into a chair in front of the desk.

"We pray first, son. Then we talk." Bruce was as good as his word, looking up at last at Barnabas. "Now, you have concerns. You have never not been able to talk with me."

"I know, Dad. This time is difficult." Barnabas pulled his upper lip down over his teeth for a moment. "What I'm going through? What Aubrey went through? I think it was to get at you."

"At me?" Bruce frowned. "Explain, son. I'm not quite following you."

Barnabas handed over the paper that he had been rolling in his hands. "This. I came up with this list last night. Baird and Branigan stopped in. They have a lot of the same names. We were talking about it and all came to the conclusion that someone was after you and through you, possibly the Foundation."

"I see." Bruce reached for the paper, not taking his eyes from his son. "And you think that I wouldn't listen to you?"

"No, not that, Dad. I'm just not sure that we're on the right track. That's all."

"I have had the same thoughts. John and I have been going back over everyone that we have had dealings with that were hostile or wanted something from the Foundation that we were not willing to give." Bruce studied the list. "I see you have a good memory. Some of these are recent but I can see two that go back to when you were a baby and I had just set up the Foundation. They didn't think my money should be used for charity. They wanted it for their own use. One of them? He actually sued to stop us."

"He did? Who?"

"Sam Pine. That's someone who has always hovered around the edge of our Foundation. We suspect that he has tried things over the years." Bruce sat back, thinking when a grim look came over his face. "He's from up north, son. Not too far from where you found Aubrey."

"Then he would know Jeremy. Aubrey said Jeremy is notorious in that area. In fact, he has been banned from one town. We stayed there when I first rescued her, assuming that we would be safe for at least a day or so."

"You were likely correct to do so. Now, we need to find out who all he is related to. I am sure, knowing his character, that he will not bring in outsiders to do his dirty work."

———

"Emma or Kataleen, I would think." Barnabas pulled out his phone, irritated at the incessant vibrating. "It's Kataleen. She has sent an email to both of us, she says. We need to look at it."

Bruce was already pulling up his email program and as he read the email, his face grew grimmer.

"We're on the right track, son. Now, let's get together with the fellows and see what we can do to solve this. Your first Christmas with Aubrey is in a few weeks. I don't want this overshadowing it."

Barnabas rose and followed his father to the conference room, pacing along the edge of the room, reading the whiteboards and realizing just how far the fellows had come. He stopped at the logic problem and gave a grim smile. They had nailed the person, he thought. Now to speak with Dallas. He turned his head as he heard footsteps.

"Dallas? You're here?"

"I am. Will has sent me, once more, to work from here. Davy will be in and out, he says. He's working on other cases. Given what happened to you, Will wants this solved. And no, we're not favouring you because of the Foundation. The public relations officer is putting out a statement later today."

"They are? I'm surprised. I'm not that important."

"But you see, Barnabas, you are. You have not heard the praise and conversations that we have had since it broke in the news about you. You don't realize the impact that you and the Foundation have in our community and from here to other areas. Someone is trying desperately to bring you and the Foundation down. That includes destroying your father.”

“I know. I was about to call you. Here.” Barnabas handed over the papers he had been holding. “This is what we have come up with. This particular man? He’s been after Dad since I was small.”

“That’s a long time.”

“It is. He has had years to plot and plan and refine his revenge.”

Chapter 41

Looking around at the ladies who had gathered in her apartment, Aubrey shook inside. She wasn't used to this, she thought. At one time, it would not have mattered. She would have welcomed them. But now? Going through what she was? She felt that she was putting everyone in danger and that she hated.

Neasa had been watching her closely. "Aubrey, do you mind if we pray first? It's how we usually start. We share if we have specific concerns or know of specific concerns. Today? That would be you, Barnabas, and his parents."

"It would be." Aubrey looked down, not wanting to see pity on the face, missing the looks of caring and compassion. The ladies knew what she was going through. They had all been there.

Ker spoke. "Aubrey, you have heard our stories. We know, to a certain extent, what you are facing right now and will likely face. We want to bathe you in prayer, for wisdom, for peace, for understanding, and for courage."

Aubrey nodded, biting at her lip as she tried to control her tears. "You have no idea what this means. I was so isolated for so long. I shut down, just because that was how I could keep sane. He took that from me. I want him to answer for that. And I have no idea how many others he did this to."

"And he will. The fellows are working on it. We want to as well. We can bring a different perspective to it. We've done it in the past." Guenivere looked around.

"That's okay. We can, but I think this time it needs to be a joint effort." Cadee spoke from where she had stood for a moment before she sat back down. A puzzled frown was on her face. "I don't get why."

"It's about the Foundation." Devaney spoke up, Berneen nodding her agreement. "We have always felt that something was left unresolved in whatever we went through. Neasa, they never did find out who ran you two down. Breck is next to Barnabas here. If he had been removed, who would have taken over that position?"

Neasa stared at her. "They would have had to hire, and whoever it was could have brought in someone no one would have suspected." Her phone was out as she sent off a text message to Breck. "He'll bring it up with the fellows."

Aubrey finally sat back, refreshed from the fellowship of prayer with the ladies and looked at them all. They are all so different, aren't they, Lord? Yet they fit together so well. I can see Your hand in all that.

"Fynn? You were working on ideas for the lobby for Christmas?" Imly looked at her.

"I was. I have some thoughts but it's not my building. It's ours. The fellows will not likely care what we do but we need to keep it simple and tasteful. It's an office building as well as a residence."

"And that we can do." Jaxcy reached for the plans. "Oh, I like these. You're an artist, did you know that? Hagen. Here. Take a look." She handed over the papers.

"Fynn? These are wonderful. I know the fellows will help with setting up the trees. Artificial or natural?"

"I would say artificial. That way it's easier to maintain them." Fynn looked around, happiness on her face. "You know, this is the first Christmas that we are all married. It's special. We all have plans I am sure, but we need to plan an afternoon or evening when we get together, just to do that without any thought of what we've faced or are facing."

"Oh, I like that idea." Muir raised a hand. "I volunteer to organize it if no one else wants to. Once we decorate, we can plan. Buffet? Finger foods? Fruits and veggies?"

"Yes!" Ennis turned to Aubrey who was sitting beside her and hugged her. "I am so glad you are here. You are the one who we were missing. Now, let's set aside those plans and work on solving this."

Aubrey blushed and then shrugged. "Except we have no idea who." She was on her feet, heading for the door. "Let's find the fellows and see what we can do to help."

The men looked around as the ladies entered, even as Barnabas was on his feet heading for Aubrey. He swept her into his arms, holding her tight as she shuddered.

"Sweetheart?"

"Barnabas, love. We've come to help. We want this over because we have plans for a building party for Christmas. And this cannot interfere with it. How do we make that happen?"

The men exchanged glances even as their wives drew up chairs beside them. They watched the ladies, seeing the determination on their faces. Dallas stood back, his eyes on his friends. He was glad that they had found their special helpmeets but he was just a bit envious. Aubrey watched him, catching the wistful look on his face, and began to pray for him, asking that God bring him that special lady.

Chapter 42

The man stood watching the ladies the next day as they shopped, Aubrey kept carefully in the centre of the group. He was frustrated. He needed to grab her to get to Barnabas, but that wasn't happening. His boss was unhappy. That person wanted whoever it was that had beaten Barnabas and left him to die.

Aubrey looked around, feeling the eyes of her. Ker was watching her and spoke quietly.

"Being watched?" At Aubrey's nod, Ker looked around, her gaze finding the man. "Listen. Stand with your back towards that way. I see him. I want to take your picture but I'm really taking him. Then I can send it on to to the fellows." She was as good as her word, the other ladies nodding their agreement.

Aubrey was frustrated. "I can't even shop without being followed. I'm still a prisoner, only I don't know who my captor is."

"No, you don't." Locklin spoke from beside her. "We all had that. So we know somewhat of what you are saying. It was different for each one of us, though. Now, how be we find somewhere for lunch? I for one am starved."

"The diner. They have a room we can use." Muir had her phone out, putting in a request. She looked pleased as she pocketed her phone. "It's free and we are welcome to use it. That's what is so nice about this town. They care about people."

Hagen stared at her. "Muir, what did you say?"

"What? That we had the room?"

"No." Hagen shook her head. "About this town. That they cared about people. That's what we've been missing. The Foundation has driven that for so many years. I know we've talked about someone wanting to take down the Foundation. My question is why? Who have they stopped?"

Ennis nodded. "That. That's so true. Ask anyone and they'll have been helped by the Foundation or know someone who has been. Cadee? Any word from your parents?"

"No. Running the shelter they should have heard something and haven't. Dad thinks whoever it is has brought in someone from out of town. There are strangers around here all the time, just given the location of our town near the canals and the lake."

"Too true. Let's sort ourselves out and head out for the diner." Berneen linked her arm with Aubrey. "Aubrey, you stay in the middle of us. That way, he, whoever he is, has to get through all of us. And we are a formidable group when we're together and angry." Her comment was met with howls of glee and agreement.

Seated in the restaurant, Aubrey shrugged out of her jacket and looked around. This is what I need, Lord, these friends. They are helping me to live once more. I was so afraid and uncertain when I arrived.

Barnabas, bless his heart, has tried, hasn't he, dear Lord? But sometimes it takes a feminine perspective to help balance everything again."

Barnabas sat back in his desk chair. He had just finished a very disturbing call with someone that he didn't know. How that woman had known to reach out to him, he wasn't sure. He looked down at his notes and then rose, looking for Dallas.

Dallas looked up as Barnabas dropped down beside him, his notes hitting the table. He tilted his head to watch his friend.

"Barnabas?"

"I just got off the phone with a Lucy Logan. She contacted me out of the blue. I have no idea who she is or if she is even legitimate. She had quite the story to tell. Here. These are my notes. Read through them."

Dallas took them, scanned them, and then read through them. "She has a lot of information, doesn't she?"

"She does and I would like to know how." Barnabas blew out a breath. "She is adamant that someone is trying to nab Aubrey again, with the goal of getting to me. They get to me, then they get to Dad and through Dad, you know where."

"We know. I spoke with Abe this morning, just to get his perspective. He is concerned but given that we have no real information as to why or who, he is suggesting that you be very cautious where you go, be cognizant of those around you and your surroundings. The same goes for Aubrey. As much as you two want to be out and about on your own, and I totally get that, he has suggested that someone be with you. Some of the fellows here. Myself. The security people.”

“That really throws a damper in spontaneous romantic dates.” Barnabas sounded glum. “I know why and I can understand that. I just don’t have to like it.”

Dallas began to laugh. “The fellows would tell you the same thing. Let me see what I can find on this woman.” He looked up as Bruce sat beside him. “Here, Bruce. Do you know this woman?”

“Who? Her? Sure. She applied to work here when we first opened up, but something was off about her. Her words didn’t match her lifestyle. Is she the one?” Bruce looked over at his son.

“She called today, Dad, out of the blue. Read my notes, if Dallas will share. Tell us what you know about her.”

Bruce thought back over the years to Lucy Logan. He frowned as he remembered how desperate she had seemed to land the position. He had not had a good feeling about her, something was off, and he had gone to the board, knowing that they would either confirm or recommend what they needed to.

The board had gone over all the applicants and Lucy’s had been questioned. One of the older men on the board, long since gone to heaven, had shaken his head. Not her, had been his comment. She says the right words but her lifestyle belies them. She was into the shady side of life as he had called it. They had prayed over the applications and made their choice. As he recalled, she had not taken it well, swearing revenge on him. He and the board had discussed her reaction, documented it, prayed about it, and moved on.

Bruce looked at the two younger men and sighed. What the board had thought was in the past was coming back. How did they now deal with it?

Chapter 43

Lucy Logan stared at the Barnabas Foundation website, anger growing inside her. They had destroyed her life by not hiring her all those years ago. That's what she had been told. She didn't doubt now that the person telling her this was correct. At the time, she had shrugged and decided whatever. She had moved on until about four years ago when she was approached and offered a large sum of money to bring down the Foundation in any way that she could. She had stared at the money, shaken her head, and walked away. The man kept coming back, the money offered increasing to the point that she had reached out a hand, taken it, and then walked away, to plan just how she could do that.

Lucy had looked at all the men employed by the Foundation and decided to work through them all. What she had not counted on was that someone else was after the men as well. That had frustrated her. By the time that she arrived at Breck's turn, she was angry. She had waited for Barnabas, knowing he was the one that she needed to go after. By that point, it really didn't matter if he died or not. She had not planned on him leaving town and then coming back with a wife. How dare he! She had put her life on hold, she thought, and never married. How dare he go on with his life! After what his father and the Foundation did to her. Alcohol and drugs fuelled her anger. She didn't understand that she was being used and likely would not even care if she did.

Rising, she headed for her vehicle, trying to come up with a plan, any plan, that would bring Barnabas to her. She decided that somehow she would find Aubrey and use her to get to Barnabas and then use Barnabas to get to Bruce. She drove around the Foundation property for two or three days at different times of the day, finally picking a spot to stop. Lucy pocketed her keys and walked towards the gardens, sneaking in without as much fanfare as she could.

She watched the ladies and men and the small children as they roamed the gardens, her eyes on Aubrey as she moved around with the ladies. This frustrated Lucy that she was never out there on her own. How could she get to her?

Then, one late afternoon, Lucy found her moment. Aubrey had stopped in the gardens, her hands touching the lamps that would soon be lit before she turned. She was restless, Aubrey thought, expecting something bad to happen. It just hadn't yet.

Hearing a footstep, Aubrey spun and began to back up from the woman in front of her. She studied her, seeing the ravages of the rough life Lucy had lived, of the alcohol and drugs that had ruined her beauty, the rage that kept building in her.

"I'm sorry. I don't think that you belong here. You need to leave." Aubrey continued to back away, hoping to make it to the path where she could run for the building.

Lucy simply shook her head, a gun appearing in her hand.

"Stop moving. You're not getting away from me."

"I'm sorry. I don't know who you are, but you don't belong here." Aubrey still moved backwards as she could, judging the steps that she could take with the way the gun was wavering.

Lucy strode towards her, the gun now pointing at Aubrey's head. Aubrey froze, seeing the instability in Lucy.

"No, you're coming with me." Lucy grasped her arm and pulled her roughly with her, her eyes searching for anyone who was coming to help. "I said, you're coming with me." Her gun jammed into Aubrey's side, stopping the younger woman's struggles to release her. Lucy stopped by her car. "In. I said, get in." She shoved Aubrey in, the gun pocketed and a syringe instead in her hands.

Aubrey began to please, begging that she be let go. That she didn't know who Lucy was or what she wanted. Lucy gave a cackle of glee, knowing that she had Aubrey where she wanted her.

"I want you. I want Barnabas. And then I want Bruce. He has to pay."

"Pay? For what?" Aubrey tried to find a way to escape but Lucy blocked her line of flight and Aubrey knew that she would never make it across the console and out the driver's door before she would be shot.

"I'll tell you that when I'm ready." Lucy studied her impassionately and then studied the syringe. A swift movement on her part and the syringe needle plunged into Aubrey's arm.

Aubrey struggled to get away, her vision darkening as the drug took effect. She slumped down, her head sagging forward, even as Lucy slammed the door and then walked to her own door, opening it to slide in. She drove away rapidly and aimlessly, her eyes on the road ahead of her, not worrying about being seen. In her mind, she had done nothing wrong.

She pulled into a garage in a remote location, turning off the vehicle and then moving to unlock and open the door to the house. Lucy returned to pull open the passenger's door, staring down at Aubrey. She tugged her from the car and then dragged her across the garage floor, up the stairs and to a room on the first floor. Aubrey was shoved into an antique wooden armchair.

Reaching for the rope that she had left handy, Lucy tied Aubrey securely to the chair before she turned away and headed for the kitchen. She reached a shaky hand for the bottle that was on the first shelf of the cupboard. She needed that drink and a large one at that.

Chapter 44

Turning from his desk, Barnabas pulled out his phone about the time that Lucy had appeared. He sent a quick text off to Aubrey, just to tell her that he loved her before he headed down the hall. Shoving open the door to the conference room, he paused, his eyes on the fellows. Most of them were there, he could see. Brady was absent, off on duty. Burnie had to be out of town that day to meet with his publisher. The rest were there. He could tell that they had been busy.

He walked about the whiteboards, reading what had been discovered. Barnabas paused as he came to the name of Lucy Logan and frowned. She really is involved in a lot of things, crime and whatnot, isn't she? He hazarded a guess that Dallas knew a lot more than he could tell, and that was okay with him. It was how it was to be.

Bradon approached him, his head tilting to watch him.

"Barnabas?"

"Bradon?" Barnabas turned to him. "You fellows have been busy. I see that you have found a lot of information."

"We have. And still are. Kataleen and Emma are sending on what they can and copying it to Dallas." Bradon turned to watch Dallas. "He's not saying much."

"No, he can't." Barnabas turned to watch him. "He's burning out, Bradon, not just from us."

"He is. I asked him how long he planned to stay a detective. He just looked at me, a bleak look on his face, and shrugged. He's hurting about something and he doesn't feel comfortable enough to share."

"No. All we can do is pray for him." Barnabas excused himself, moving away to stop and speak with each of the fellows, ending up at Breck's side.

"Breck? They're quitting in good time?"

"They are. We're making sure of that. This cannot affect their brides, even though the ladies are willing to let them." Breck handed Barnabas a mug of coffee. "How are you doing, my friend?"

Barnabas shrugged. "I'm not quite sure, to tell you the truth. I worry so much about Aubrey and she is doing the same about me. It's making it tough. And now this with Dad? That has added an extra layer to our stress. God is there, but sometimes it is hard to remember that."

"It is, Barnabas. It is." Breck looked around. "We all know that, even though this is much worse for you, just because it affects the Foundation." He paused, his eyes on his own mug. "Listen. Can you and Aubrey come for dinner tonight? You need time to just relax and maybe, just maybe, take your mind off this for a while."

"I'll ask her." Barnabas sent off a quick text, staring at his phone with a frown on his face. "That's odd. She hasn't responded to my other text. And she always does right away." He spun, almost running from the room, the fellows looking up and then at Breck as he followed Barnabas at a rapid pace.

Barnabas flung open the apartment door, rapidly searching and not finding Aubrey. Where is she, he thought? He spun, running for the door and then outside, Breck at his heels. They searched the grounds, not finding her, before Barnabas slid to a stop, his hand reaching for Aubrey's phone, Breck's hand on his wrist stopping him.

"No, Barnabas. We need to call it in." Breck looked up to find Dallas watching from just behind them. "Dallas?"

Dallas nodded. "I called in it. They're on their way." His hand out, he led Barnabas back from the area. He nodded as Bradon appeared, his dog, Kade, at his side. "Go ahead, Bradon. See what you can find."

Barnabas stood near the edge of the building, his arms wrapped around his chest, eyes not moving from the officers and techs that searched the area. Bruce stood beside him, his arm around his son's shoulders. Elizabeth had been out there and he had sent her back in to wait where it was warmer. The fellows from the building had gathered around them, quiet, grim looks on their faces. Aubrey would not be the first one to disappear from the building. They had all prayed that she wouldn't. God was in control, Baird commented, even when they could not see it. They knew the ladies and Anna and Amy were gathered in the chapel, petitioning the gates of heaven.

Bradon reappeared, waiting for Dallas to approach him. He shook his head.

"There was a vehicle waiting there. Kade tracked Aubrey to there. She disappeared into it."

"Again? I'll send the techs that way." Dallas turned to watch Barnabas. "We need to get him inside. This dampness is not going to help him."

"No. I'll see what I can do."

"Bradon?" Dallas called after him, waiting until he turned back. "Say nothing. Let me do that/"

"I will. He may not ask."

"He will. Trust me. I would in his position." Dallas turned to find one of the techs and a patrol officer that he could send that way.

Barnabas looked up as Bradon approached, hope dying in his heart at the look on Bradon's face. He drew a deep, shaky breath before he spoke.

"Let's go on in, Dad, and find Mom. I need her." Barnabas staggered as he turned, his father's arm out to come around him and lead him away, away from where his beloved Aubrey had last been.

Bruce shared a look with Bradon, who simply shook his head. Bruce nodded. She's gone, and now we have to find her. Lord, why? I don't understand but I do know that you are in control.

Chapter 45

Elizabeth sat beside Barnabas, a hand on his back as he leaned forward, his head buried in his hands, elbows on his knees. For once, like Bruce, she was unable to make it all better for him. That disturbed her. She looked up as Will appeared, shaking her head at him. Will nodded before he sat beside Barnabas.

Barnabas turned his head to watch his friend, not quite sure why Will was there and not Dallas.

"Will?"

"I'm here as a friend today, Barnabas', not as an officer. That's Dallas' job right now. His and Davy's. He said that they would be in shortly." Will prayed for his young friend. "What can you tell me?"

"Not a lot. I was working all afternoon. Aubrey had planned to do some reading she said. She can't get enough books now. I sent her a text late afternoon, just before I went to the conference room. She didn't respond and that's when Breck and I went searching." Barnabas drew in a deep breath. "Where is she, Will?"

"We'll find her, son." He watched as Barnabas shook his head and then stood, staring at the floor.

"But will she still be alive? It's to the point that I don't think that anyone cares whether she lives or dies. Not us, but whoever it is. They seem determined to bring as much hurt as they can and don't care who it destroys." He walked away, the fellows gathering around him as they stood, heads bowed to pray for their leader.

Will watched him, a frown on his face.

"He's right, Will." Bruce spoke from where he stood. "I don't think they care if someone lives or dies. And I wish I knew why."

"The Foundation. You've used your money as a trust to help. People resent that. They want the money for themselves and they really don't care how they get it. Right now? I would say that Aubrey is hidden somewhere close, where they can watch the activity here."

"Have you found Lucy Logan yet?"

"No, we haven't. Not that I am aware of. The detectives may have but we are swamped right at the moment with cases."

"I know, Will. I know that. Whatever it takes to help let the Foundation know. I don't want to be put to the forefront and ahead of anyone else if it's a matter of life and death."

Will stood, his hand on his friend's shoulder. "But it is, Bruce. It is. It is a matter of life and death for Aubrey and likely Barnabas. Not one of the officers will have it any other way but that they work on this. They are working on it in their own time. I have said not to, that they need the downtime. It doesn't matter. You and your organization have done so much for our town. This is how they pay you back."

"I didn't do it for payback. You know that."

"No, you didn't, but the town feels a debt that needs to be paid, one of so many. Even the council has approached me, asking what they can do. This will accelerate that giving. Take it as it is meant."

"I will." Bruce looked around. "I need to go and call the board."

"It's been done. I talked to John. They are heading this way, Bruce, just to be with you."

"Thank you, Will." Bruce stood for a moment, unsure of what to do, before he headed for the chapel, pushing the door open and then entering to sit at the back, not disturbing the young ladies who had gathered.

Neasa looked around and then moved to sit beside him, her arm linked with his, as she prayed for him. Bruce was loved by all in the building and it hurt them all to see the suffering that the family was undergoing.

Chapter 46

Two days later, Barnabas looked up as he heard footsteps approaching him. He had been searching, on his own, not letting the fellows know that he was. They knew, without being told. One of them always followed him, keeping him in sight, but not close enough that it would cause him distress that they were putting themselves in danger. The man who stood in front of Barnabas was well-groomed. Barnabas frowned, not knowing who it was.

"Mr. Carey. I need you to come with me."

"I don't think so. I have no idea who you are." Barnabas stood and moved back, towards the street where he could run if he had to.

"Oh, I think you will. Check your phone." The man waited patiently as Barnabas pulled out his phone.

Drawing in a deep breath as he stared at the photo, Barnabas looked up in anger.

"Where is she? What did you do to her?"

"I did nothing to her. That's not to say something more won't happen. That's why you come with us." The man pointed towards a luxury vehicle. "In there." He reached out a hand. "Your phone."

His hand tightening on it, Barnabas almost refused before he reluctantly handed it over. He watched as the man simply tossed it into a trash container before he pointed once more to the vehicle. Given no choice, Barnabas headed that way and was soon seated. His eyes searched the area, seeing Branigan approaching the trash container. Good, he thought. He'll grab my phone. Dad has the password to get in.

"Where are we heading?" Barnabas shifted to watch the man.

"Not your concern. Not yet." He drove seemingly in random circles before he pulled to the side of the road. He handed Barnabas a bandana. "Put this on. And once it is on, you don't move it. Your wife's life depends on how well you follow instructions."

Branigan fished the phone from the garbage and then stood staring after the car, his mind memorizing the license plate number before his phone was out and he was making that call all of them had dreaded. Now not only was Aubrey missing, so was Barnabas. The next one would be Bruce. That was a given, he thought before he began to pray.

Breck approached him, a frown on his face.

"Branigan? I got your call. What happened?"

"I was staying back just like we agreed on. Barnabas was sitting there when some well-dressed man approached him. Barnabas ditched his phone, got into some high-end vehicle and they disappeared."

"Did you recognize the man or the car?"

"No. But I got a picture of it as well as a description and plate number. I have his phone."

"Okay. I think Bruce can access it." He looked around. "Are you done here?"

"I am. Can you give me a lift back to my truck? Then I'll follow you home."

Thirty minutes later, the two men stood in Bruce's office, watching as he sank back into his chair, his face white.

"Barnabas? He just went with him?"

"I'm sorry, Bruce. He did. I wonder if Aubrey was threatened or you." Branigan handed over the phone. "This is his. He threw it away. I think he saw me."

Bruce reached for the phone. "He did? Then he knows we have it." He hesitated, spending a bit of time in prayer before he unlocked the phone and then searched the text messages. "Here. Oh, no!"

Breck reached gently for the phone and turned it, a deep breath drawn as Branigan muttered under his breath. The photo showed Aubrey slumped in the chair, her arms bound to it. They could not get a sense of if she was alive but assumed that she was.

"I need to get this to the investigators, Bruce. Do I have your permission?"

Bruce nodded, unable to speak. He rose, stumbling somewhat and Breck's hand went out to steady the man he considered a second father.

"I need to find Elizabeth. She needs to hear it from me."

"I'll go with you. Branigan?" Breck looked over at him.

"I'm heading for the fellows. We're not leaving that room until we come up with some answers. The ladies have already told us that is what they expect." Branigan was away, stopping outside the conference room to pray before he entered.

A sudden hush dropped over the room and several of the men rose, their eyes on him.

"It's bad, fellows. Barnabas was just taken. I saw it and could do nothing." Branigan held up his phone. "I have photos that we can work with." He searched the room, finding Dallas heading his way. "Dallas?"

"Send it to me. I'm heading in." He was gone before anyone could respond.

Chapter 47

Staring at her husband, Elizabeth shook her head even as the tears started and her hands covered her mouth. Bruce swept her into his arms and just stood, holding her as she sobbed. He had no answers for her. Not yet.

The ladies in the chapel with Elizabeth watched in horror before Neasa's head was down and she began to petition for the couple's safe return. The others picked it up one by one. When they finished and raised their head, the older couple was gone. Muir looked around.

"Okay, ladies. This is what we expected but prayed would not happen. We put our plan into effect. Group 1, you're on for supper and late-night snacks. Group 2, we're on in the morning. And in the meanwhile, we work our own searches and try to keep our fellows' spirits up."

Two days went by before Bruce was approached by the same man as he walked across the parking lot from John's office. He was forced by gunpoint into the same vehicle as his son had been and driven away, no one around to see anything. The man had made sure of that. He had been promised good money if that happened, and he could always use the money, he thought.

No one was aware that Bruce too had gone missing until Elizabeth looked at the clock and realized that it was mid-afternoon and Bruce had not appeared for lunch. There was no answer to her phone calls or her text messages. Frantic, she ran from their apartment, heading for Breck, meeting him coming towards her.

"It's Bruce. He's gone."

"Elizabeth? Bruce?" Breck's hands on her arms stopped her.

"I just realized that he had never come home for lunch. I can't get an answer when I call or text him."

Breck's face grew grimmer as with his hand on her arm he directed her to the conference room.

"Fellows? Bruce has disappeared. Where was he, Elizabeth?"

"He had a meeting with John early this morning. He said he'd be home by noon. I didn't realize it until just a few moments ago." She took the handkerchief that Brennen handed her, wiping at her face and then twisting it in her hands.

"Brennen? Find Dallas." Breck's voice was quiet even as Brennen had nodded and walked away rapidly, heading for the lobby so that he could call in private.

Dallas had appeared, not surprised that Bruce had disappeared. He had been the target after all, hadn't he? John was there as well, aghast that Bruce had disappeared as he left their meeting. He had been in touch with the board, who would gather at the building to make plans.

The fellows had taken a look at Elizabeth and then dove back into their research. Blair had been on the phone to Emma, begging her to help. She had simply stated that she was, that she was sending on more information and did they need Abe and her to come?

Chapter 48

A few hours after she had been abducted, Aubrey had roused and begged to use the facilities. The sedative had sent nausea roiling in her stomach. She had rinsed out her mouth after she had been sick, staring unseeingly at herself in the mirror before she was dragged back to her chair and shoved down into it. A bottle of water had appeared as well as a sandwich. Shaking her head at the food, she had simply downed some water. Her arms were once more bound to the chair. She had wept, pleading to be let go, but silence had met her demands.

This had been the routine for the next day or so, Aubrey sleeping from the sedatives that she was slipped in her water. She didn't hear the curses of the woman as she paced, hateful glares sent her way. She also didn't hear the woman on the phone, demanding that Barnabas be found and brought to her.

Barnabas was pulled from the car and then shoved forward, his shoulders moving away from the push, and through the door into the house, his blindfold still in place. He stumbled as he hit the tile floor and had to fight to keep his balance. He felt the hand on his back leading him to another room where he too was shoved into a chair and bound. The blindfold was roughly pulled from his head. He blinked and squinted as he tried to once more become accustomed to the light.

He squinted as the light became bearable and he looked around. He gave a cry and fought to free himself, spying Aubrey slumped in a chair across the room. The rough rope dug into his wrists and ankles. There was just no way that he could free himself.

"Let me go. Let me go to her!" Barnabas was pleading, he knew. The only response was a gun barrel jammed against his temple, stilling his movements.

There was the tapping of high heels and Lucy appeared, a sneer on her face. She studied the younger man before she handed over another wad of cash.

"There. Now, hide until I need you again. It will not be that long." She watched as the man carelessly stuffed the money in his pocket and left before she turned to Barnabas. "So, Carey. You are now in my control. Good. It's been a long time coming." The alcoholic haze that she was in had her convinced that she was in control and that she would win. She didn't see the determination on his face to somehow free himself, free Aubrey and leave. Only, he had no way of knowing where they were.

Two days later, Barnabas looked up as he heard footsteps. His heart sank. He recognized his father's. Dad, they got you. I was praying that they didn't.

Bruce sat where he was told to. He had not been surprised that he was not blindfolded. He had recognized the property and knew that the men of the building had been right all along. They had insisted that the Logan property was still kept up and that Lucy lived there. Boys, I apologize and I will do that in person when I come home. Only, Lord, I don't know that I will.

Lucy stared at him and began to laugh, an evil laugh that turned into a cackle and then choking. Her lifestyle was not conducive to good health. Bruce studied her, seeing the changes that life had made in her. He sighed. Even if she had been given the work, he didn't think that she would have lasted. Sin had pulled at her and pulled her hard.

Lucy paced around them, her words muttered and incoherent before she abruptly walked away. Bruce could hear the clink of a bottle and grew suddenly afraid for his son and daughter-in-law. What was she planning? Nothing for their good.

"Dad?" Barnabas kept his voice low.

"Son? You're okay?"

"I am. I mean, I haven't been treated the best." His eyes went to Aubrey. "It's Aubrey. She's been kept sedated, I think. She doesn't even know that I'm here."

"I see. You haven't been able to loosen your bonds?"

"Not really. I tried." Barnabas looked over at his father, his eyes narrowing at the satisfied look on Bruce's face. "Dad?"

Bruce shook his head. "Not now, son. Let me think about this for a moment." Bruce continued to twist at his bonds, finding them loosening. He had not been bound very well, he thought, and wondered at that. He didn't think the man really cared but Lucy would. His right hand slipped free and he quickly moved to untie his left wrist.

On his feet, his pocketknife out, he slashed at Barnabas' bonds and then at Aubrey's, gathering Aubrey into his arms before he pointed at the front door with his chin.

"Out that way. Lucy's drunk. I think I heard her hit the floor"

"I think you're right. Dad, let me have Aubrey."

"Not yet, son. Hurry. I don't know if anyone else is around."

The men headed for the nearby trees, walking as rapidly as they could, deep into the area before Bruce paused. Barnabas was beside him, his hand on Aubrey's face, and then her wrist.

"She's sedated, Dad. They kept doing that. She kept being sick and begged them not to give her any water. Lucy forced her to drink if she refused." Barnabas looked up, fear for his young wife on his face. "How do we get home, Dad? And do you know where we are?"

Bruce looked up at the deepening night. "I do, son. It's the old Logan place, not too far from home. Here, you take your wife." Barnabas reached for her and then watched as his father bent over, to pull a slim tiny phone from his shoe.

"Dad?" His questioning voice caught Bruce's attention.

"Will and I talked. We thought they would try and take me. They did. We came up with this." He held up the phone. "It's a pay-as-you-go. He found one as small as he could. Now, let's pray that I have enough signals to get help." Bruce punched in Will's number and waited.

"Bruce?" Will's voice over the phone carried to Barnabas.

"Will, they made that attempt. They had me but I managed to escape. I have both Barnabas and Aubrey. We're in Weaver's woods, near the old Logan place. What's that? The Logan place? Yes, it's the one. The boys were right when they said it would be where she was. But we had no evidence, now did we?"

"No, we didn't. Hang on for a moment." Will's voice softened as he turned to speak with someone. "Davy's on his way. Brady's with him. Doc is waiting in the infirmary for you three."

Chapter 49

Doc stood back at last, his eyes on the young couple before he moved to the hallway, finding the whole building family waiting, children included. Heath and Hannah had been begging for their Aube, in tears because they couldn't see her. He looked around at the men, seeing the worry, concern, and determination on their faces. On the ladies' faces, he saw the same but also the peace that only God could bring.

"Doc?" Breck spoke for the group.

"Bruce is okay. Just some abrasions on his arms. Barnabas is the same. He tells me that he tried his best to escape the ropes but he just couldn't. Aubrey is sleeping. She roused for a bit and then went back to sleep. She was kept sedated, Barnabas says."

"Praise God that we have them. But do we know why?" Blair looked around.

"Not yet. Will said Dallas and his team are working on that. Something about arrest and search warrants and needing to confirm facts." Bruce stood facing them, back to the room where his son and his wife lay, his arm around his own wife. "Thank you, men, ladies. Your prayers protected us, I have no doubt. I recognized the man. He's a hired assassin, among other things. I have no idea if Lucy is the one who hired him or not." Bruce gave a weary sigh. "How be we head to the chapel? Elizabeth, I know you're staying. I'll be back." He kissed her quickly before he moved among the building family, hugs to all, and then headed for the chapel, Buckley and Locklin on either side of him.

Will stood for a moment watching before he turned to Dallas.

"Get their statements. Then, take tonight and get some rest. I think that you won't be getting a lot in the next few days."

"I will. Just a question. They were in the Logan place? Didn't we search there?"

"We did. It looked as if someone had been there and then locked it up to be away for a time. We need to speak with that patrol officer again." Will's phone was out as it vibrated and he paled. "We can't do that."

"We can't?" Dallas was confused. "I don't understand."

"They just found his body next to his patrol car. A head shot, the responding officer said."

"The assassin?"

Will gave a grim nod. "I would guess that. Don't let those three out of the building. I don't care if you have to lock them into a room and keep the key. They'll be after them." Will walked away, heading for his vehicle. This was one part of the job he hated. Having to notify next of kin of a death.

Barnabas slipped from the bed that he had been lying on and headed for Aubrey, a kiss on her cheek, and her hand in his as he bent over her, watching her beloved face. He saw the whiteness of it, the black circles under her eyes, and the hollow cheeks. He frowned. She must have been sick a lot, he decided.

Doc stood watching him before he approached, an arm around the young man who he loved like a son. His prayer whispered in the quiet of the room.

"Doc?" Barnabas looked up at him. "Is she okay?"

"I would think so. We'll let the intravenous run and then decide if we need to do another one. I suspect that we will. Brady took the blood we drew into the hospital lab for me. We'll know if there is anything off. She's in a natural sleep, son."

"I know. I just worry. She didn't eat and barely drank the water. She tried to refuse and Lucy made her drink, even as she sobbed and begged her not to." Barnabas knew that he would never forget his helplessness in being able to help her.

"It will haunt you, Barnabas. We'll pray for you about that." Doc's hand rested on his shoulder. "I'll be back. Anna was heading up to heat some soup for you two."

"Aubrey won't eat. She'll think that she's still a prisoner." Barnabas rested his hand on her hair.

"We'll see. I'm sure that you can convince her."

Doc stood with his back resting against the door before he looked up. Dallas stood in front of him.

"Doc?"

"They have survived. We'll need to find someone that they can speak with. You've gotten their statements?"

"I have. Even Aubrey's although she faded on me just as she finished and signed it." Dallas shook his head, fatigue hitting him.

Doc watched him. "Head off to bed, Dallas. You've been burning the candle at both ends. As Will said, take the time tonight to sleep."

"Thanks, Doc. I will."

Chapter 50

Aubrey stared at Barnabas, shock on her face. She shook her head. There was no way that Bruce had been able to get free and walk out with them.

"That can't be right. You were tied up, weren't you? And I know that I was. Besides I couldn't stay awake. I don't think that I even knew you were there."

Barnabas wrapped her in a hug. "I love you so much, sweetheart. My heart broke when I couldn't get free and get you out. Dad somehow was able to loosen his bonds and walked us out."

"I don't believe you. I mean, I know it's possible, but where was that woman?"

"It happened, sweetheart. We think that she passed out and dropped to the floor in the kitchen. We heard what we thought was a body hit the floor."

"Is it over?"

Barnabas shook his head, sorrow on his face. "Not yet. They're still working on search warrants and arrest warrants, Dallas said. He's not sure how long it will take. They need to round up everyone, he says, before we're safe."

"And we're prisoners again, aren't we? Kept in our home. I need to get out, Barnabas. I can't handle being locked up, even for a day or so. I just can't." She wept against him, feeling his kisses on her hair.

"Then, we won't. We'll take all the precautions that we can, but we will not be kept in." He set her back from him, his hands on her arms, his eyes searching her face.

"So, how do we do this, then?" She watched him, not quite sure that she should have spoken.

"We go out and about. Today, we go out for lunch. It's Saturday. I was told not to work until Monday. Then, tomorrow, it's church and we will be there."

"Of course, we will. We need that." Aubrey stepped back, heading for her coat. "If we're going out for lunch, then let's go. Fast food or diner?"

"I think the nice Italian restaurant. And yes, you are dressed just right." He reached to stop her, kissing her thoroughly, a finger drawn down her flushed cheek when he finished.

Bruce watched them head for Barnabas' truck and shook his head. He figured that they would make the decision that they had and feared for them. He turned to find Elizabeth beside him.

"They have the right idea, love."

"I know. I just fear for them." He looked down at her. "I suspect that they are heading out for lunch. Care to do the same?"

"With my best beau? Any time." Elizabeth tucked her hand around Bruce's arm. "Where to?"

"I don't really care. That Italian restaurant? We haven't been there since we came home."

"No, we haven't."

Bruce paused as they entered the restaurant and began to laugh. Barnabas looked around and grinned.

"Running away, Dad?"

"Escaping, son? I didn't know that you were heading here."

"Nor me you. Shall we take separate tables or pretend that we are on a double date?" His grin widened as he looked down at Aubrey. "Care to double date with my parents?"

Aubrey studied him, studied Bruce, and then looked at Elizabeth, finding the older woman barely containing her mirth. She gave a deep pretend sigh. "If we must, we must." She reached for Elizabeth's arm. "Seeing as they are so undecided, how be we find a table?"

Bruce and Barnabas shared a look before they broke out into laughter.

"I think that we just got told, Dad." Barnabas followed the ladies, holding their chairs while they were seated and then moving them into the table before he sat himself. He looked around the restaurant, nodding at friends and acquaintances before his eyes rested on a man seated near the front of the restaurant. He excused himself as he sent off a quick text to Dallas, who he knew was looking for that very man.

They watched as an officer entered and approached the man, speaking with him and then leading him from the building. Bruce caught the look on his son's face and nodded. He reported him, didn't he, Lord? Is this why we were here today? To find him? If this is why, thank you for bringing it up.

Aubrey turned to Barnabas before a frightened look covered her face. Barnabas started to turn to see what she was looking at but a prick from a knife against the back of his neck stopped him. He saw the fear on the other patrons and prayed, harder than he had in the past.

"Look who we have?" Lucy Logan's slurred voice sounded in his ear. "Just the people I wanted to find. I don't know how you escaped, but you won't again. Never again." The knife shook against Barnabas' neck. "You will pay for not hiring me. You and that Foundation that you are so proud of."

"Lucy? You know as well as I do that you were not qualified for that position. You would never have stayed. Your lifestyle would have drawn you away."

"That's what you think. I can stop the alcohol and the drugs at any time." Her face twisted with her words and then twisted more, fear showing on it, as a hand reached for her chest and then she dropped.

Bruce was on his feet, calling for someone to help, before he knelt beside her, a hand reaching for her wrist before he bent his head, ear to her chest, and then hand to her neck. He stood, his arm reaching for his wife and drawing her away. Barnabas moved away with him, Aubrey tucked up against him

"Dad?"

"She's gone, son. God has chosen this route for her. He has spoken. We will never likely know exactly what drove her." Bruce turned as he heard the sounds of the emergency vehicles and pulled his family out of the restaurant.

Chapter 51

A day later, Will and Dallas faced the building family, gathered in the conference room. They had sorted through the details, finding it not quite as it had seemed. They had worked all night, Dallas and his team and the techs sifting through evidence. There were still some details that needed to be finished but they could finally say what it had all been about.

Buckley had been watching them and then stood, calling for attention. He stated simply that they needed to spend some time in prayer. When they had finished, they looked around, their eyes on Barnabas and Aubrey as they sat, his arm around her, his parents near them. A sense of relief filtered through the room. This was it, wasn't it, they all thought? The end of it?

Dallas stood at the front of the room, his eyes on Will before he looked at Bruce and then Barnabas and Aubrey. He swallowed hard, knowing that this was the end for the investigations for these men. He had not known them well, other than for speaking at church when it had all started with Baird but as he had worked with them, he had gotten to know each one and their ladies and valued their friendship and walk with God. He had come to some decisions about his own life and this was the final investigation, he had decided. He had spoken to Will, who had questioned him, prayed with him, and then given his blessing.

"Aubrey, we'll start with you. Jeremy has confessed that he was paid to keep you captive, to interfere in your relationship with Barnabas. Someone had been watching you that closely. We'll come to who. When things started to heat up about two years ago, he was ordered to cut all contact off between you two. What was not expected was that Barnabas would go looking for you, enter the house and then disappear with you, marrying you in the meantime. He was paid well for his trouble, I must say, but he is now through as a lawyer, has been for quite some time. His son was not part of it. He decided on his own that you were his. You suspected that Jeremy tried to keep you two apart and you were correct in that.

"Barnabas? Now it's your turn. Lucy Logan was behind it, but there was someone behind her. I'll come to who it was. You were right when you suspected that two different people were involved in what went on with the fellows. And you are correct in thinking that it was escalating with each one. The ATV that ran down Breck and Neasa? It was Lucy herself on it. She apparently thought that if she took him out, you would be more vulnerable. She left a detailed diary of everything she did, and everyone she hired. We're working on sorting through that and arresting each one. You all can rest easy that we have that solved.

"As to why she was after you? Your father was correct in thinking it was because she had been turned down for work here. But someone had approached her, trying to bring down the Foundation. From her diary, we have determined that she kept refusing until the money was just too much. Alcohol and drugs had taken over her body and mind. Her thoughts were becoming more and more muddled. She would have faced multiple charges, including murder and kidnapping among others. You are not the first that she went after.

"Bruce? What can I say? I wish that we could have solved this before your son and his wife were hurt. But we couldn't. Lucy is not the one who hired the men who attacked Barnabas and left him for dead in the parking lot. I'll come to him, I promise. Lucy was after you for revenge before you shoved her aside, in her words. But she was not the only one. I am sure you will recognize the name."

"Dallas? Who is it?" Bruce exchanged a look with Elizabeth. "You speak as if I know him."

"You do, Bruce. Only too well." Dallas paused, praying as he did so. "The name? A well-known entrepreneur in the area."

"William Thomas?" Bruce's voice was quiet even as Elizabeth's hand tightened on his.

"You are correct." Dallas nodded, his eyes not leaving Bruce's face. "He was infatuated with Elizabeth and had determined that she would be his. Only she never looked at him. Never spoke with him. You and Elizabeth were friends for years, best friends through high school and university. Am I correct?" He nodded as Bruce looked at his wife. "He felt slighted and thought that she only wanted anything to do with you because of your money. It didn't matter that the money was inherited and that you invested wisely and with the Lord's leading to increase its value. When you set up the Foundation with its goal of being an encouragement and aid to others less fortunate, he again thought that this was a slur again him. His mind became warped in this thinking. All he has accomplished in his life has been in competition with you, or so he thought. He married but his wife left him in less than a year, not telling him that she was expecting. She moved from the area and he has had no contact with his son. That he blames on you as well. We have had him assessed. He will not face any charges. He has been committed under a mental health assessment. He also has cancer, which is terminal."

Bruce grew sad as he listened. "I never really knew him. We had a couple of high school classes together, but we never had anything to do with one another in them. Our interests ran differently. Would it have made any difference if I had?"

Will spoke up from where he stood behind Bruce, drawing the attention to himself.

"I spoke at length with him, Bruce. He was becoming more and more incoherent as time went on. It would not have made any difference. In fact, from what he did say and that I am not at liberty to divulge, it would have made it worse. He has admitted that he went after all the men, including your son, as a sick kind of revenge. In his mind, you ruined him. And you took the woman that he wanted."

"God protected us." Bruce hugged Elizabeth and then turned to Barnabas. "I'm sorry, son."

"For what?" Barnabas' brow wrinkled as he looked at his father

"For involving you in this. A mad man as we used to say, out for revenge."

"But you didn't know, Dad. No one did, did they, Dallas?"

Dallas shook his head. "No one. He kept it hidden. He did become prominent in the community but never in a church. He refused to step inside one, not even for a funeral. I'm sorry that we didn't catch him before he put all of you through what he did."

"It's not your fault, Dallas." Aubrey spoke up. "It's life. It's how God has worked. He has taught all of us something different, something that we needed to learn. For myself? He has taught me how to live. With help from my love." Aubrey turned to Barnabas. "We can become angry, bitter, or let God fill us with His peace. I had so many days, weeks, months and years to work through this. I choose to live, to let God work through me."

Buckley's voice raised in a hymn of praise, the others adding their voices before he prayed. He looked around when he finished before he just hugged Locklin. Lord, Aubrey is so wise. You have taught us so much. Thank you, Lord.

Six months later, Barnabas stood in the newly-dedicated playground and family activity area that Neasa's brother, Nevin, had created for them. He was so thankful, he thought, for the friends who had become family. Friends from all over Canada. Even some of the ladies, he thought, came from outside the area. He turned as Breck stopped beside him.

"I never thought when we were teens and talked about what we wanted to do that both of us would be working here." Breck smiled.

"No, I never did. I wasn't going to come and work for the Foundation, you know." Barnabas grinned before he grew pensive.

Breck laughed. "I know. It wasn't in my plans either. God had other plans for us." He looked around at the men. "And to think that this all started with that strong impression you had about finding orphans who all shared your initials and hiring them to work for you. To send them out as ambassadors of encouragement to the community."

"And that has worked out so well. I hear nothing but praise from their employers and their volunteer coordinators. Having the ladies join us has added to that. It has made us a family."

"A family that keeps growing." Breck smiled. "I wanted you to be the first to know after my parents.

Neasa and I are adding to our family." He nodded to the play area. "This is going to be used well."

Barnabas reached to hug his life-long friend, a prayer uttered for them. "That's great news, Breck. I am so happy for you." He watched as Breck moved away before he reached for Aubrey who had approached as he prayed. "Happy, sweetheart?"

"I am, love. I am. All those years that I thought I had lost? God was working in me, fitting me to become the helpmeet that you needed."

"He was. Enforced study I guess you could say." He stood, his arm around her, content as he watched, naming each couple and the little ones that had blessed the families. Muir and Burnie were almost parents, he thought, as were Brady and Fynn. He turned to Heath and Hannah, smiling as they waved at their Aube. She was still important to them, right up there with their parents.

Baird and Berneen, Benen and Cadee, Blair and Devaney, Bradon and Ennis, Brady and Fynn, Branigan and Guenivere, Brandon and Hagen, Brendon and Imly, Brennen and Jaxcy, Brody and Ker, Buckley and Locklin, Burnie and Muir, Breck and Neasa, he thought of each one as he named them. Thank you, Lord, for each and every one of them.

Bruce approached his son, dropping a kiss on Aubrey's cheek, and then laying a hand on his son's shoulder.

"Okay, son?"

"Double okay, Dad. You and Mom just got in?"

"We did. We tried to get here earlier but the traffic was backed up coming from Toronto. I wish that we had been. I have seen the playground is already in use." He grinned at his son.

"It is, Dad." Barnabas bit at his lip, an action that Bruce recognized as uncertainty on his son's part.

"Something that you need to tell me, son?" He looked over at Aubrey to see her blushing. Elizabeth stood with her arm around her daughter. He smiled as he remembered her adamant words that Aubrey was a daughter in love, not in law.

"There is, Dad. Aubrey and I are taking off for a couple of weeks, and I promise. This time we are not running for our lives or across the province to keep alive." He looked down at her, to find her eyes on him, confidence in him showing. "When we come back, I need to talk to you about something new that Aubrey would like to set up. A music program for the little ones and whoever in the community would like to take part. She feels burdened about this."

"That's a good idea, son. Aubrey, just get me your proposal and I'll put it to the board. I doubt that it will be refused." He studied the two. "But that's not all."

"No, it's not, Dad." Aubrey had taken to calling them Mom and Dad. "I don't have my parents. I wish that I did. They would make wonderful grandparents." She paused, blinking away the tears, not seeing the look of amazement and then joy the older couple exchanged. "You two will. You have shown it so many times with the little ones." She stopped, unable to continue.

"What my sweetheart is trying to say, Dad, is that the love of my life and me will be parents by Christmas. That makes you grandparents. And you can't say no."

Bruce blinked rapidly. "Not that we would." He hugged the two, watched as Elizabeth did and then hugged the three of them, a prayer raising for them.

Late that night, Barnabas found Aubrey curled up in his favourite chair. He lifted her and then sat back down, cuddling her close.

"Did you ever think we would go through all this?" She tilted her head to look at him, accepting the kiss he dropped on her mouth.

"Not at all. That day I took off? All I wanted was to know if you were okay and if you still wanted anything to do with me. I didn't dream that we would have our own adventure."

"I prayed so hard for someone to find me and rescue me. Your face was always the one that I saw. Thank you, love, for being my knight in shining armour. And for teaching me how to live again."

They grew quiet, their eyes on the flickering flames of the gas fireplace that Aubrey had lit. They were with the one that God had meant for each of them, although it had taken time for that to happen.

Thank you for picking up the story of Barnabas and his love, Aubrey. Who knew that Aubrey was the one that had shadowed his life throughout the books? Some of the ladies had guessed. Learning to live once more was what Aubrey faced. Barnabas was there to provide the encouragement that she needed, to help teach her to do just that.

It is the end of a series, the end of the adventures of the Barnabas Foundation family. It has been a challenge to write, but each story has had to be told, to lead to this one. Friends from previous books and series have walked in, at just the right time. I miss the guys from *His Guardians, The Heart of a Lion, A Touch of His Garment, Under His Wings,* and *The Haven of Rest.* The friends have added to the story, moving it sometimes when it was stilled.

We are all prisoners in some way to something. God can and will open the door of the prison and free us. We just need to ask. He has promised us that. We can rise up with the eagles and fly above the storms of life. It doesn't mean that Christians don't face danger, sickness, and death at the hands of others. Sin sees that we do.

We are called to be encouragers to those around us. It is difficult, especially in 2020 when we are facing the COVID-19 pandemic and life is restricted. It sometimes is just a kind word that helps.

As I end the series and look to what comes next, Dallas is quite vocal about his story. He was to be only a minor character in a book or two, just to be the investigator. His role grew until he became an important part of the story. This has happened with so many of these men and ladies. A minor character, such as Muir's Granny, or Darbie and Hailey and Hollie, and how can I forget Heath and Hannah, such sweet little ones.

Let God have all your worries and cares. He loves you so much. As I write, I am listening to Christmas carols and reminded again of His great love and His desire that we live for him.

God bless.

Ronna